SLAM BOOK FEVER

"Biggest Flirt," A.J. read aloud from a slam book. His eyes ran down the page. Jessica felt her stomach doing flip-flops. "Wow," he said. "Ten votes for Jessica Wakefield." Everyone at the table laughed, except for Jessica, who felt her cheeks burning. A.J. looked at her curiously. "That sure doesn't seem right to me," he said warmly, staring straight into her eyes.

Jessica looked away. She couldn't believe how happy it made her to hear him say that. Did that mean he liked her? She hoped so! Jessica knew no one in the world would believe it, but she was in love. She was so much in love that she felt like a totally new person, and all she wanted to think about was A.J.

"Hey, look at this," Aaron said, taking the slam book from A.J. and flipping ahead to the Crystal Ball category. "Future Couples . . . Olivia Davidson and Jeffrey French."

"Oh," Ken Matthews moaned. "Watch out, Liz!"

Everyone laughed Elizabeth.

"And look what's and A.J. Morgan!"

This exclamation silence. Everyone looked nervously from Elizabeth to A.J. to see what their response would be.

"That's pretty flattering," A.J. said with a grin, and the tension broke. Everyone laughed again, including Elizabeth.

Everyone but Jeffrey—and Jessica, who stared at her sister with a look of abject horror in her eyes.

SWEET VALLEY HIGH

SLAM BOOK FEVER

Written by
Kate William

Created by
FRANCINE PASCAL

BANTAM BOOKS
TORONTO · NEW YORK · LONDON · SYDNEY · AUCKLAND

RL 6, IL age 12 and up

SLAM BOOK FEVER
A Bantam Book / September 1988

Sweet Valley High is a trademark of Francine Pascal.

Conceived by Francine Pascal.

Produced by Daniel Weiss Associates, Inc.,
27 West 20th Street
New York, NY 10011

Cover art by James Mathewuse.

ISBN 0-553-27416-3

Published simultaneously in the United States and Canada

Bantam Books are published by Bantam Books, a division of Bantam Doubleday
Dell Publishing Group, Inc. Its trademark, consisting of the words "Bantam
Books" and the portrayal of a rooster, is Registered in U.S. Patent and
Trademark Office and in other countries. Marca Registrada. Bantam Books,
666 Fifth Avenue, New York, New York 10103.

PRINTED IN THE UNITED STATES OF AMERICA

O   0 9 8 7 6 5 4 3 2 1

SLAM BOOK FEVER

One

"Jessica!" Amy Sutton cried, her gray eyes flashing. "Come over here!" She motioned to the empty seat beside her in the crowded cafeteria of Sweet Valley High.

Jessica was relieved that Amy had saved her a place, and she hurried over and threw herself dramatically into the seat. "Phew," she sighed. "What's going on here? Why's it so crowded today?"

"I don't know, but it sure can't be the menu," Lila Fowler said with a sniff, poking at that day's entree—Special Chicken—with a look of distaste.

The table of girls erupted into giggles. "Not like Chez Victoire, huh?" Cara Walker said. The

1

restaurant she was referring to was one of the most exclusive and high-priced French restaurants in Los Angeles, and of course everyone knew that Lila had eaten there the weekend before. It was a long-standing tradition to needle Lila about her father's incredible wealth. As the only daughter of a computer tycoon, Lila was used to what she called "certain fineries." Apparently Special Chicken wasn't one of them!

"We've been waiting and waiting for you, Jess," Maria Santelli said. "Amy's been promising to tell us about slam books, but she made us wait until you got here."

"Slam books?" Jessica unwrapped her sandwich. "What are they?"

Amy tossed her blond hair back over her shoulders. "I told you before. They're exactly what Sweet Valley High needs. In fact, I can't even believe you guys don't have them here yet. Everyone had them in Connecticut."

Although she had been born and raised in Sweet Valley, Amy had moved to Connecticut for most of junior high and part of high school. Recently her mother had been hired as a sportscaster for a TV station near Sweet Valley, and the family had moved back. Already Amy had gotten a reputation for being, among other things, boy-crazy, slightly bossy, and somewhat snobby.

2

"Go on, then. Tell us what they are," Jessica said.

"OK, here's the deal." Amy was obviously enjoying being the center of attention at the lunch table. She cleared her throat, paused, and slowly looked at each girl around her. "Everyone who wants to take part buys a notebook. Any notebook is fine, but we can all get the same ones. The best ones, like the ones we used back in Connecticut, are those black-and-white speckled ones—you know, composition books. You write your name on the inside cover. Next you divide your book up into the girls' part and the boys' part. And then you start inventing categories. Best Looking, for instance, or Most Popular. We had lots of different categories: Best Sense of Humor, Biggest Flirt, Best Kisser, things like that. You get the idea. You invent a bunch of categories, then swap books with someone else. Then you fill in names in their book and swap again. At the end of the day, you return the notebook you've got to the girl whose name is on the inside cover."

"Wow, Amy, this sounds great!" Lila exclaimed.

"I don't know," Cara Walker said skeptically. "It sounds kind of confusing to me. What's the point, Amy?"

"The point," Amy said, "is to have a good

time! The books are incredibly fun, you guys. And it's totally anonymous. There's no way anyone can find out if you've said—well, like, say you think Jessica's the most flirtatious girl in school, and you enter her in that category. And then some other people do. And so on and so on. Well, wouldn't it be fun when we all sat around reading them and saw how many people thought she was the biggest flirt?"

Jessica's blue-green eyes narrowed. "Who thinks I'm flirtatious?" she demanded.

"That was just an example," Amy said. "But do you all get the point?" She rummaged around in her book bag. "Look. Here's a slam book from my school in Connecticut. You guys won't know any of the names, but you can kind of get the idea from this."

She passed a black-and-white notebook around the table, and everyone took turns looking at the categories.

"This is great." Maria giggled. "I love the category Least Down-to-Earth!"

"Yeah," Lila said. "I like the Best Dressed category. This is going to be great, Amy! Let's get notebooks. I'm ready to start."

"But who's going to take part?" Maria Santelli asked.

Amy shrugged. "Whoever wants to. The way

4

it happened at my school in Connecticut was that just a few of us had slam books at first. Then it caught on, and soon everyone had one—at least, all the girls."

"What a cool idea!" Jessica exclaimed. "Just think, we're all going to know exactly what everyone thinks of us!"

Jessica was certain that she was only going to find out good things about herself. Or, at least, things she already knew. She wouldn't be surprised if she were described as most popular. After all, she *was* a co-captain of the cheerleading squad *and* the president of Pi Beta Alpha, the exclusive sorority at Sweet Valley High. Or maybe even most beautiful. . . . Jessica was off in a reverie and barely noticed when Elizabeth, her twin sister, set her tray down on the table.

"Hey, can you guys squeeze me in? The lunchroom is really crowded today," Elizabeth said.

"Sure," Amy said, sliding her tray over. "I was just in the middle of telling everyone about slam books." Her eyes twinkled. "You'd better prepare yourself, Liz. This is going to be the biggest thing to hit this school in a long time."

"Slam books? What are they?" Elizabeth asked.

It took Amy a few minutes to go over what she'd already said, but this time several of the others, especially Lila and Jessica, interrupted her, adding categories they had just devised.

"Like, we could have Least Likely to Go Out on a Date Before the Year 2000," Jessica cried.

"Or, Most Likely to Always Be a Millionaire," Lila offered.

Elizabeth unwrapped her ham and swiss cheese sandwich and took a bite. "Sounds potentially mean, you guys. What happens if people read things about themselves that they don't like?"

Amy and Jessica exchanged a glance. It was just like Elizabeth to come up with a *sensible* objection.

"Look, Liz. It's just for fun. No one's going to get hurt," Lila said.

Elizabeth shrugged. "It just sounds like the sort of thing where someone's going to end up feeling crummy." She took another bite of her sandwich. "You've got to remember, I've had some experience with this sort of thing from writing the 'Eyes and Ears' column for *The Oracle*. You wouldn't believe the kinds of suggestions people drop in the box. If I didn't edit them. . . ." Elizabeth wrote the gossip column for the school paper, and she took her job very seriously. She tried never to print any piece of gossip that would hurt a fellow student.

"It's just for fun, Liz. Don't be such a spoilsport," Jessica said.

"Uh-oh! It's twin against twin," Lila said with a giggle. "Round twelve."

At this, everyone laughed, including Jessica and Elizabeth. They knew better than the others what Lila meant. It wasn't easy being part of a pair that was identical on the outside and totally opposite on the inside!

When it came to looks, *identical* was the word for Jessica and Elizabeth. With their sun-streaked blond hair and their perfect size-six figures, the twins were exactly alike in every detail—from their wide-set, blue-green eyes to the tiny dimple each showed in her left cheek when she smiled.

But when it came to personalities, it wasn't hard to tell the girls apart. Jessica thrived on change and excitement. She loved being a part of the action, and that's why she was a cheerleader and a member of the sorority. Whatever the latest trend, Jessica was sure to be part of it. She went through fashions, friendships, and flirtations with lightning speed. And she just couldn't understand how her twin could be so steady, so serious, so conscientious.

Elizabeth loved school—even the schoolwork part. She adored working on the newspaper and hoped one day to be a writer. She liked to take her time with whatever projects she started, and she liked to know, when they were done, that they were done right. She also liked spending time alone, or just relaxing with Enid Rollins, her best friend, or Jeffrey French, her steady boyfriend.

"Look," Elizabeth said, taking a sip of milk, "the slam books will probably turn out to be perfectly harmless. I just thought— "

"You're right," Jessica interrupted. She jumped up from her seat. "I want to get one right away!"

Everyone at the table laughed again. Nothing could be more characteristic of the Wakefield twins. Elizabeth just wanted everyone to be cautious, to think the idea over, to make sure no one would get hurt in the process.

But not Jessica. Jessica was full steam ahead, and nothing in the world would stop her now!

"Liz," Jessica gasped, hurrying up to her twin after school. "Cheerleading practice was canceled. Any chance you'll give your favorite sister a ride home?"

The twins shared the use of a red Fiat Spider. But Jeffrey didn't have his car that day, and Elizabeth had made plans to take him home. "Sorry," she said, "but I told Jeffrey that I'd drive him home. And he's got some work to finish up at the *Oracle* office first."

Jessica's face screwed up with impatience. As

far as she was concerned, Elizabeth and Jeffrey spent far too much time together. She couldn't understand why neither of them was interested in dating anyone else. She couldn't imagine anything more boring.

"Maybe I could drop you off, Jess, and then go on. If you don't mind coming with me to get Jeffrey from the office and—"

"Do you know who that guy is?" Jessica interrupted, pointing to a tall redhead fumbling with his locker.

Elizabeth shook her head. "I've never seen him before. Why?"

To Elizabeth's surprise her twin blushed, an honest to goodness *blush*.

"I'm going to go find Lila and try to get a ride from her." And with that Jessica was off, without another glance at the redheaded guy.

Elizabeth smiled as she turned down the hall toward the newspaper office. Leave it to Jessica, she was thinking. With that girl you really never knew what was up. If that redhead knew what was good for him, he'd watch out from now on.

The door to the *Oracle* office was open, and Jeffrey and Olivia Davidson were inside, deep in conversation. Olivia, a pretty girl with hazel eyes and thick, slightly frizzy hair, was the arts editor for the paper. She was well known around school for being slightly bohemian, more artsy than most of her classmates. Jeffrey was a staff photographer, and they had done a number of projects together in the past few months.

"Hey, guys," Elizabeth said, setting her books down on the table. "What's up?"

"Oh, I'm just trying to talk your boyfriend into co-editing the new literary magazine with me," Olivia said. About a month earlier, Olivia had asked Elizabeth to co-edit the literary magazine she was starting. But between writing the "Eyes and Ears" column, writing regular features for *The Oracle*, and keeping up with homework, Elizabeth knew she wouldn't have time, so she had turned Olivia down.

"First, you said no," Olivia went on, "and now Jeffrey's trying to. I think he's afraid he'll end up spending all his time working. Then he won't have any time with you."

Elizabeth smiled affectionately at Jeffrey. "Oh, is that so?" she said. Jeffrey's eyes crinkled up as he smiled back and leaned over to give her a kiss.

"You got the story I submitted, didn't you?" Elizabeth asked Olivia. "When's the first issue coming out? I can't wait to read it!"

"Well, I'm hoping in three or four weeks. I got a lot of submissions, and I've already picked out what I want to use. And your story is one of them, Liz. Then I've got some poems and cartoons, and Jeffrey's agreed to do a special photo essay and the cover. Right, Jeffrey?"

"Right." Jeffrey smiled. "I figure it's the least I can do."

"Mr. Collins is going to help me set up stuff with a printer and all that." Olivia tucked a strand of hair behind her ear. "But I can tell I'm still going to have my hands full." Her voice quavered slightly, and she added, "Probably a good thing, too."

Jeffrey glanced at her. "What do you mean?"

Olivia shrugged. "Oh, you know. Just that sometimes it's good to have too much to do."

Elizabeth studied Olivia closely. Was it her imagination, or was something wrong? Olivia seemed a little distraught, and her voice sounded slightly unnatural, almost as if she were stubbornly trying to present a cheerful front.

Jeffrey had to go down the hall to the darkroom, so he left the two girls alone. Elizabeth watched Olivia quietly for a minute. "Are you OK, Olivia? You seem kind of distracted. Maybe you've been working too hard," she said.

Elizabeth had always liked and admired Olivia, but had never spent a lot of time with her other than working on *The Oracle*. Olivia had been dating Roger Barret Patman for quite a while and spent most of her time with him.

11

Olivia bit her lip. "Actually, Roger and I . . . well, lately we've been having some pretty serious problems. I've been upset about it. That's why I've been throwing myself into work, I think. I'm afraid to face what's going on with the two of us."

Elizabeth was extremely surprised. Roger and Olivia having problems? She couldn't believe it. They seemed so perfect together. True, the couple had gone through some rough times when Roger had been adopted by his uncle, Henry Wilson Patman, one of the richest men in Sweet Valley and the father of one of the snobbiest, most gorgeous members of the senior class, Bruce Patman. But that was all ancient history. Roger came from a poor family. When his mother died of heart disease, he was shocked to discover that Mr. Patman, who had helped pay for his mother's medical expenses, was in fact his uncle. Roger turned out to be the illegitimate son of Mr. Patman's own dead brother. The revelation, and its subsequent change in Roger's life-style, had made things hard for the couple. At first everyone feared that Olivia wouldn't fit into—or be accepted by—Roger's glitzy new family. But they had worked through it and ever since had been very, very close. Elizabeth was shocked now to discover there was friction between them.

"Oh, Olivia. I'm so sorry."

Olivia nodded. "Thanks, Liz, I think things are going to be rough for a while. That's one reason I'm glad I've got this new literary magazine to keep me busy." She tried hard to smile, but Elizabeth could see how sad Olivia was.

When she drove Jeffrey home, Elizabeth asked him if he had noticed that Olivia and Roger were having problems.

Jeffrey shook his head. "Olivia never talks about stuff like that. She's all business," he said. "But I guess she has seemed kind of upset lately. Why? Did she tell you they're not getting along or something?"

"Yeah. She said they're having serious problems, but she didn't elaborate. She's definitely upset, though," Elizabeth said.

"Wow. That's too bad," Jeffrey said softly.

"I know." They had stopped at a light, and Elizabeth put her hand over Jeffrey's. It was scary to think a couple they both liked so much was having problems. She hoped Olivia and Roger could manage to work out their problems.

She could tell Jeffrey was a little bit scared, too. He squeezed her hand tightly. Elizabeth was thinking how lucky they were to be able to talk things through.

Jeffrey gave her a big hug when she stopped

the car at his house. "I happen to love you, Elizabeth Wakefield," he murmured.

Every time Jeffrey said that, Elizabeth felt like the luckiest girl in the world. It made her feel less anxious about Olivia and Roger—at least for the moment.

But she found herself wondering about the couple as she pulled up into the driveway of her own house. She knew Olivia would be strong no matter what. But she hoped that what seemed like serious trouble now would soon blow over.

Two

By the next day half a dozen girls had slam books. Amy had organized a trip to the stationery shop after school on Monday, and everyone bought the same kind of notebook—black-and-white speckled covers with ruled paper inside. Each girl had carefully written her name on the inside cover, divided her book into two sections, and invented a number of categories for each. So far Jessica, Lila, Cara, Robin, Maria, and Amy had the notebooks. But so many other girls asked about them on Tuesday that Jessica was sure they would catch on in no time. A number of girls from the sorority said they were going over to the stationery shop after school to get composition books. Amy had definitely started a new fad!

"OK, let's get started," Amy said at lunchtime. "Jess, give me your notebook, and I'll give mine to Lila. Lila, swap with Robin . . ." Soon the notebooks were all jumbled up.

"Hmm. The first category in this book is Class Clown," Amy announced.

The first category in Jessica's book was Most Conceited. Under it she wrote Bruce Patman. Jessica had always thought the dark-haired, handsome senior was arrogant. She had dated him briefly a long time ago and never really forgave him for the terrible way he had treated her.

After she had gone through the entire book filling in names, Jessica swapped books with Robin. The first heading in this book was Best Couple. And the first entry underneath was Elizabeth and Jeffrey.

Jessica smirked. She thought Elizabeth and Jeffrey were the most boring couple, but she didn't think they deserved another heading all their own. She flipped to another page. Biggest Brain was the category. She filled in Peter DeHaven's name. Perfect. He was the science genius who had already been accepted to MIT, early admission.

The girls spent the rest of the lunch hour

passing their slam books around, reading each other's entries, and giggling. Under the heading Most Fascinating New Male in Lila's book, two girls had written in A. J. Morgan.

"Who's A. J. Morgan?" Amy demanded.

Lila pretended to be shocked. "You mean you haven't seen him? The big, tall, handsome redhead from Atlanta?"

Amy laughed. "Nope. Sounds like I've missed something special. What's he like?"

"He's gorgeous," Robin said.

"Really hunky," Maria chimed in. "But he seems kind of shy."

"Yeah," Lila agreed, brooding. "I tried to talk to him a few times yesterday, and he was nice enough and everything, but he didn't really respond. Maybe he only likes southerners."

Jessica fiddled with her notebook, her cheeks pink. So that was his name—A.J. She wanted to ask the others for more information, but she felt inexplicably—and uncharacteristically—unsure of herself.

"What's A.J. stand for?" Amy asked.

"Adam Joseph. He's an army kid," Lila went on.

Jessica shot her a look. How come Lila knew so much about the new boy? "It sounds like you two talked for quite a while," she said. "He

17

may not have responded, but you were sure trying!"

Lila shrugged. "Why not? You know my philosophy, Jess. If you see something great, why not grab it?"

Jessica's heart started to beat faster. She couldn't believe Lila had already moved in on this guy!

"But he didn't seem very interested in me," Lila admitted.

"You guys," Amy protested. "You're forgetting about the slam books."

"Look," Robin said with a giggle, pointing to an entry in her book. "Jessica wins Biggest Flirt!"

"She's down in my book for that, too," Cara said.

Lila leaned over to pat Jessica on the shoulder. "See? You can't claim you're not getting any credit, Jess."

Jessica felt her face burn. "I'm not a flirt," she objected. "I don't know what you guys are talking about."

Amy started to laugh. "Come on, Jess. *You*—not a flirt? Are you kidding?"

Jessica was beginning to get annoyed. "I'm not kidding," she said flatly. "I don't happen to think of myself as flirtatious."

The table fell quiet for a minute. "Jess," Cara

said a bit timidly, "what would *you* call it if it isn't being flirtatious?"

"I don't know what you're talking about," Jessica retorted hotly. "Just because I happen to have a lot of guys as friends . . ."

"You mean just because you torture a lot of guys who are crazy about you," Amy shot back. "And get them to think you like them when you couldn't care less about them . . ."

Jessica didn't answer for a minute. Was that how her best friends saw her? As a big flirt?

Well, if that was true, she certainly wasn't going to let them go on thinking that. She intended to change her personality drastically—and fast.

A. J. Morgan walked by, and Lila nudged Amy. "That's him," she said. Jessica felt her face redden. She didn't even look up at A.J. as he strolled by.

Well, one thing was for certain—she wasn't going to act like a flirt around *him*!

Jessica was on her way to cheerleading practice on Tuesday afternoon when she caught sight of A.J. talking to Aaron Dallas, co-captain of the soccer team, and two seniors on the basketball team, Paul Isaacs and Jason Mann. OK, she told herself. This was it—a perfect chance to go

19

over and introduce herself. She could pretend she had to ask Aaron a question about the basketball schedule.

Why did she feel so shy at the thought? Jessica couldn't believe she was acting this way. *Come on,* she told herself sternly. *This is ridiculous!* And holding her head high, she strolled over to the lockers where the boys were standing.

"Uh—hi, guys," she said, not with her usual ease and poise but with an embarrassed, almost silly smile.

"Hey, Jess." Aaron greeted her with a grin. "Do you know A. J. Morgan? He just moved here from Atlanta," he added.

Jessica looked at him and, to her horror, felt herself blushing.

"There's two of them, A.J., so don't get confused," Aaron warned the new boy. "Both of them unbelievably pretty. Right, Jess?" He gave her a friendly wink.

Jessica's blush deepened. Why did Aaron have to pick that minute to tease her? And why had she come over in the first place? A.J. would think she was a total moron. She lifted her eyes for a split second and looked up at him just long enough to see he was studying her curiously.

"A.J.'s joining the basketball team," Aaron

went on. "Perfect timing, too. The team really needs a new center." The boys fell back into discussing sports, and Jessica, feeling slightly idiotic, just listened. She kept waiting for an opportunity to jump into the conversation but couldn't find one.

Finally A.J. turned to her, his dark eyes attentive. "Which way are you heading?" he asked. "I'll walk a little way with you. I've got a meeting with the coach, but not for ten minutes."

Jessica's heart started to pound. "I—uh, I'm heading to cheerleading practice." *Great conversationalist*, she told herself sarcastically. *At this rate A.J. really is going to think I'm a moron!*

"How long have you been a cheerleader?" he asked her. It was obvious he was trying to think of things to keep the conversation going, since she wasn't being much help!

"Oh, for ages," Jessica said, taking a deep breath. "What about you—how long have you played basketball?"

A.J. had a low, gravelly voice. "Not all that long. Everyone always thought I was a natural, 'cause I'm so tall. But we've moved around a lot because of my dad—he's in the army—so I've never really had a chance to get good at a sport." He smiled, a nice natural smile. "I like baseball, though. Wait till you see me at baseball games. I turn into a total fanatic."

Jessica stared at him. *Wait till you see me.* . . . Was that promising or not? She felt she was hanging on every word he said, trying to get some sense of whether or not he was interested in her.

They walked together in silence for a few minutes, and Jessica felt herself beginning to panic. She couldn't think of a single thing to say to him! How could this be happening? Usually she was the one who chattered on and on. And now, when it really mattered, she couldn't think of one single thing to say.

"Well," A.J. said finally, shoving his hands in his pockets and looking slightly ill at ease, "I guess I should go. Nice to meet you, Jessica."

Jessica looked hopelessly at him. "Nice to meet you, too," she murmured. *How original,* she scolded herself. She had just had the perfect opportunity to get to know this incredibly cute new guy, and what had she done? Acted like a zombie. She hadn't even said *one* memorable thing the whole time they'd been talking. She had just walked beside him in mesmerized silence. What a great way to make a first impression! He'd be sure to avoid her next time they passed in the hall.

Jessica was still berating herself when she hurried into the locker room to change her clothes. Amy Sutton was pulling on a pair of khaki shorts.

"Hi, Jess," she said cheerfully as she tucked in her T-shirt. "What's wrong?" she demanded, seeing the downcast look on Jessica's face.

"Oh, nothing," Jessica said dully, opening her locker and rummaging around for her practice clothes.

"You look like you just lost the sweepstakes," Amy commented.

Jessica slipped out of her skirt and top and put on shorts and a T-shirt. "I'm fine," she said shortly. "I just had a long day, that's all."

Whatever happened, she wasn't going to tell a soul about what a fool she had made of herself in front of A. J. Morgan. She was positive about that.

Just then the locker room door opened, and several of the cheerleaders came in. Jean West, Sandra Bacon, and Maria Santelli were all talking animatedly about none other than A. J. Morgan.

"He's in my art class," Maria gushed. "And he's gorgeous, you guys! Absolutely gorgeous. Sort of cool and remote, though. He hasn't paid one bit of attention to any of the seniors in the class, even though they're all flirting with him like mad."

23

"Yeah, I saw a bunch of girls trying to hit on him at lunch today," Sandra piped up. "He seems kind of aloof. I wonder if he has a girlfriend back in Atlanta."

Jessica slammed her locker shut, her eyes flashing. She didn't want to hear another word about A.J.

"Come on, you guys," she snapped in her most authoritative co-captain's voice. "We've got a lot of stuff to run through before the game on Friday. Let's get started!"

A moment's silence followed this outburst. But Jessica didn't wait around for a response. She stormed out of the locker room toward the field.

Elizabeth was working on her history homework that night when she heard a loud knock on her bedroom door. "Come in," she called, setting her book aside.

Jessica stuck her head in the door. "Are you busy?" she asked, her expression grave.

Elizabeth laughed. "Not anymore. What's up?"

Jessica hurled herself down on her sister's bed. "Liz," she said seriously, "do you think I'm a flirt? Tell me the absolute truth."

Elizabeth bit back a smile. "A flirt?" she repeated with mock surprise. "You?"

Jessica sat straight up. "Yeah, I couldn't believe it either," she declared. "But about five people have written that down in their slam books. I can't for the life of me figure out why anyone would put me down as Biggest Flirt." She frowned and shook her head in disbelief.

Elizabeth fiddled with her pencil. "Well, I guess I can see what they mean—a little bit," she said gently. "You *do* like talking to guys, let's admit it."

Jessica tossed back her hair. "But not flirting," she protested. She was still frowning. "I don't like being thought of as a flirt. It really bugs me." *And what if A.J. finds out?* she was thinking.

"I told you those slam books might cause trouble," Elizabeth said. "Think about it. If you're this upset about being called Biggest Flirt, what's going to happen when someone invents a category that's really hurtful?"

Jessica shrugged. "They won't. I told you, Liz, the slam books are just fun. No one's going to get hurt by them."

"Then why does it bug you so much being called flirtatious?" Elizabeth asked reasonably.

"Because," Jessica said indignantly, "it isn't true!"

To her horror she felt her eyes filling with tears. Jessica didn't have the faintest idea what was wrong with her, but she didn't like it. She fled from the room before Elizabeth could see that she was crying, and when she reached her own room, she threw herself down on the bed and sobbed.

Olivia drew a deep, quavery breath. She and Roger were sitting together, parked in his car in her driveway. She was trying her hardest to fight back tears.

"Roger, I feel like we're not trying hard enough. We have so much going for us. Don't you think it's crazy to be fighting all the time?"

Roger was slumped in the driver's seat. "It is. I just don't know what to do about it." He sighed. "Maybe we've gotten too serious too fast, Liv. Maybe we need to start thinking about—you know, loosening things, so we don't feel so tied down."

Olivia's eyes filled with tears. "I don't feel tied down!" she cried. But she knew there was no point in saying it. Roger obviously did.

She had known this was coming for a long time. The past few months had been nothing but arguments. A familiar pattern had established itself: Roger would do something to hurt Olivia, she would strike back or start a fight, and they would come to this point, staring miserably at each other, not wanting to break up and not wanting to go on.

Something was obviously going to have to change. But Olivia couldn't bear the thought of losing Roger. She didn't think she could stand the loneliness.

Whatever it took, she was going to fight to keep their relationship going.

Three

Amy Sutton was in unusually high spirits on Wednesday. "I guess people know a good thing when they see it," she said to Jessica. "I saw a whole bunch of girls passing around slam books this morning before school started. I can't believe how fast they're catching on." The girls were on their way to class, their own slam books tucked in their arms with their school books.

Jessica was slightly distracted. "Yeah, Amy, that's great," she murmured.

Amy didn't notice her friend's preoccupation. "I guess I deserve all the credit," she mused. "I mean, just think about it. If it weren't for me, no one would even know what a slam book *is*." She frowned. "Do you think everyone appreciates me for introducing the idea? Or is everyone going to forget it was mine?"

Jessica patted her on the arm. "We'll all remember, Amy. We'll put up a big commemorative plaque in the front hallway."

Amy ignored her sarcasm. "Just wait till you hear the great idea I've come up with today," she said triumphantly. "But I'm not going to tell you now," she added. "It's a surprise. I'll tell you at lunch."

Jessica gave her friend a look. She wondered if this slam book idea was going to Amy's head. By the time they finally made it to the lunchroom later that day, Amy was beside herself with excitement.

"Listen, you guys," she said in a stage whisper to the small group assembled in the corner of the cafeteria. "I've come up with a fantastic idea for a new section for the slam books."

Cara and Lila stared at her. "Well, what is it?" Lila prodded her.

"It's called The Crystal Ball," Amy said portentously. "It's like a glimpse into the future. See, we'll all make a whole section for it in our books, and then we can include more new categories. Like, Most Likely to Have a Million Dollars by Age Thirty."

"That's not much of a question," Lila said with a yawn.

Amy ignored her. "Or Most Likely to Get Married First. Or Most Likely to Be Famous. You know! It'll be great," she said enthusiastically.

Jessica, despite herself, had to admit it was a great idea. She could already think of a category to add—New Couples of the Future. And the first entry—A. J. Morgan and Jessica Wakefield. To her annoyance she could feel herself blushing, and she had to pretend to be studying her notebook.

Winston Egbert came over, balancing his tray with one hand. "Ladies," he said dramatically, "I've been hearing rumors of little speckled notebooks calling me Class Clown. Is this true?"

Lila rolled her eyes, but everyone else giggled.

"I think I need to see my name in print," Winston added. He pulled up a chair and snatched Jessica's slam book out of her hands. "Here it is," he said sadly. "Class Clown—Winston Egbert. Why not Most Handsome? Or Biggest Jock?"

"Uh, well, we're saving those up, Winston," Amy said.

Winston put the notebook down with a frown. "Seems like kind of a weird idea to me. Why are all the girls in this school suddenly running out and buying these notebooks? I guess I just don't understand the female mentality."

"You should get the guys into it, Winston," Amy said warmly. "What about Ken Matthews and Aaron Dallas and those guys? Don't you think they'd like to be part of this?"

"No," Winston said promptly. "But go ahead. Read me some of the entries. I want to be on the cutting edge." He pretended to glower. "I want to hear who won Best-Looking Guy so I can know the competition."

"Hey, let's put Winston in one of the Crystal Ball categories," Cara said. "How about Most Likely to Be in *People* Magazine?" She wrote in the category at the top of the page and entered Winston's name.

Winston took a bite of his sandwich. "Most Likely to Be Cutest Guy in Ten Years?" he volunteered. Everyone laughed. Winston, tall, lanky, and thin as a rail, was lots of fun to be with, but no one would call him the cutest guy.

Lila had taken Jessica's slam book and was staring at the new category under the Crystal Ball section. "New Couples of the Future," she read aloud. She furrowed her brow a little, thinking.

Winston brightened. "Winston Egbert and Christie Brinkley," he said.

"Better not let Maria hear you say that," Amy said. Maria Santelli was Winston's girlfriend.

Once again everyone burst out laughing—everyone, that is, except Jessica. She had just seen A.J. come into the lunchroom. And as long as he was around, she couldn't think about anything but him.

"Jess, what's wrong?" Lila demanded after school that day. Jessica was at her locker, rummaging wildly through her things in search of her history book.

"Nothing," Jessica muttered. But her bad mood was obvious.

Cara came up behind Lila. "Anyone want to come with me to the Dairi Burger on the way home from school?"

"Jess is fuming about something, but she won't say what," Lila told her.

Jessica yanked her history book out of the bottom of her locker, sending papers flying across the hallway. "It just so happens," she said coldly, bending down to gather up the papers, "that I'm sick of being called Biggest Flirt in people's slam books. Do you realize I've seen a couple dozen books today, and *most* of them have my name in that entry?"

Cara and Lila exchanged glances. "Well, who would *you* call the biggest flirt?" Cara asked diplomatically.

Jessica stuffed the papers back into her locker and slammed it shut. "I'd say either it would be you, Lila, or else Amy. It sure wouldn't be me," she said. The locker bounced open instead of closing, and she slammed it even harder. "I'm *not* a flirt," she added sulkily, not giving Lila a chance to protest. "Since when have you guys seen me flirting?"

Lila started to tick off on her fingers. "Remember the chef who taught the gourmet cooking class?"

"What about all those friends of Steve's from college?" Cara added. Cara dated Steven, the twins' older brother, and knew how many times Jessica had fallen for one of his friends. Or at least flirted with them.

"Not to mention Aaron Dallas, Nicholas Morrow . . ." Lila offered.

"And Alex Kane," Cara added, referring to a musician Jessica had recently had a crush on.

"And what about Jeremy Frank?" Lila demanded.

Jessica cut her off. "That was all ages ago. It's ancient history. Can't you guys see I've changed?"

Lila and Cara looked at her, then at each other. "You look the same to me," Lila said philosophically.

Jessica's eyes flashed. "I've had it," she

34

snapped. "I'm not one bit of a flirt, and I'm sick of people saying I am."

"OK, OK," Lila said quickly, surprised by how angry Jessica sounded. "Calm down, Jess. The slam books are only for fun."

"Well, it doesn't happen to be fun for me being called a flirt. And that's final," Jessica said.

"Come on, guys. Let's go to Casey's and get some ice cream," Cara said, obviously trying to soothe Jessica.

"All right," Jessica said. But she was still mad. What if A.J. found out? He was so shy, not exactly one to like a girl everyone agreed was the biggest flirt in the whole school. If it were true that she had ever been a tiny bit flirtatious before, she vowed to herself not to be anymore, not if she wanted A.J. to be interested in her.

The three girls were heading out to the parking lot when Lila spotted him. "Look, there he is! It's A.J.! And he looks even cuter than the last time I saw him!"

Jessica's mouth went dry.

"Where?" Cara asked curiously. "Oh, yeah. I see him," she said, following Lila's index finger, which was pointing at a bright red Jeep. A.J. was standing in front of the Jeep, talking to Aaron Dallas.

"Let's go over and talk to him," Lila said.

Jessica groaned. "No way. If we're going to get ice cream, let's go get ice cream."

But there was no stopping Lila now. "We have to walk past him to get to my car," she said flippantly, grabbing Jessica's arm and marching in A.J.'s direction.

The next few moments were utter agony for Jessica. "Hey," Lila said, stopping short at the Jeep and looking at A.J. from beneath lowered lashes. "We've all been talking about you. Have you met my friends Jessica and Cara?"

A.J. looked slightly embarrassed. He glanced at Jessica, then back at Lila. "Uh, I've met Jessica. Not Cara. I'm A. J. Morgan," he said.

Aaron grinned. "See, I told you, A.J. No shortage of gorgeous girls around this town."

Lila tossed back her hair. She obviously took Aaron's comment as if it were directed especially at *her*.

Cara put out her hand. "Nice to meet you, A.J." She smiled at him. "What's that short for?"

"Adam Joseph." He smiled shyly. "But I've always been called A.J."

"Jessica." Lila nudged her. "Aren't you going to say something to A.J.?"

"Uh, yeah," Jessica mumbled, looking down

at her feet. Lila and Cara stared at her, wide-eyed.

"We're—uh, we're going to get some ice cream," Jessica blurted. Aaron and A.J. looked at her in surprise, and Lila sighed loudly.

"OK, let's go," she said. As they headed toward Lila's lime-green Triumph, Jessica shot a backward glance at A.J. She couldn't believe how foolishly she had just behaved. Well, that would show Lila and Cara that she wasn't a flirt.

"Jessica, you didn't have to make a point of it," Lila said reprovingly. "We understand you're upset about being thought of as a flirt, but you could have said something to the poor guy. You didn't have to just stand there totally mute!"

Jessica shrugged. "I told you," she said, trying to keep her voice natural, "I'm not a flirt."

Let Lila and Cara think she had acted that way on purpose. That would be better than letting them know the truth—that she *had* been acting like herself, her new self. The self that turned totally idiotic the minute A. J. Morgan was around!

Elizabeth hurried into the *Oracle* office, humming lightly. She was in a good mood. She was looking forward to going out to Secca Lake with

Jeffrey for the after-school picnic they had planned.

"Hi," she said, flashing him a big smile. He was sitting at his desk in the office, riffling through a stack of contact sheets. "You ready?"

"Ready?" Jeffrey looked at her blankly. "Ready for what?"

Elizabeth gave him a wry smile. "You're not getting prematurely senile, are you? We have a date to go to Secca Lake, remember?" She put her arms around him and kissed the top of his head. "I need some fresh air . . . and"—she gave him another kiss—"some time with you."

Jeffrey groaned. "Oh, no. I forgot all about it, Liz. What a jerk I am! Are you going to murder me?"

"Why?" Elizabeth stared at him. "It doesn't matter if you forgot. I've got the car outside. Let's just go."

"I can't." He stared regretfully at the photographs. "I promised Olivia I'd go over these and make a decision by this afternoon about which one to use for the cover of the magazine. We want to have a dummy edition together by next week."

Elizabeth stared at him. "You mean—"

Just then Olivia came into the office. "Hi, Liz!" She smiled, but Elizabeth thought she looked subdued. She was wearing one of her characteristically pretty, slightly offbeat dresses and ankle boots.

"How are things going?" Elizabeth asked, trying to hide her disappointment. She couldn't believe Jeffrey had forgotten their date and made other plans. It was so unlike him!

"Oh, I'm OK." Olivia sighed, then shot Jeffrey a glance. "If it weren't for Jeffrey, I'd be a wreck. This magazine is taking every waking second. With Jeffrey's help we should make our first deadline."

Elizabeth had really been looking forward to this date. But she wasn't going to make a big thing out of it. If Jeffrey and Olivia had work to do, that should obviously come first. "Look, I'll let you guys get back to work. Do a good job!" She patted Jeffrey on the shoulder. "We'll make it up," she whispered. "Don't worry about it."

Jeffrey smiled at her, relieved. "Thanks for being such a good sport. I'll call you tonight, OK?"

Elizabeth nodded.

It really wasn't a big deal, she tried to convince herself as she left the newspaper office. She could hear Olivia's low voice as she walked down the hall, then Jeffrey's responsive laugh. Oh, well, she thought. Secca Lake would be there tomorrow.

*   *   *

Roger stopped by the *Oracle* office to pick up Olivia at five-thirty. She and Jeffrey had been working hard, and she was exhausted. Roger was tired, too. They said little as they drove through the winding streets toward her house.

"How's the magazine going?" Roger asked her.

"Fine." Olivia tried to smile but felt tears pricking behind her eyelids. It was so painful making small talk with him when she loved him more than anyone in the world! But somehow things had just gone wrong between them. There was no denying it anymore.

Roger seemed to sense her mood. "We need to talk," he said when he pulled up in front of her house. "Liv, we can't keep this up. It's killing both of us."

Olivia nodded, her eyes brimming with tears. "I know. You don't have to say it," she choked out.

He took her hand and stared into her eyes. "I want to stay friends, Olivia, but I think it's going to take me a while. I've . . . well, I've never broken up with anyone before. I'm really not sure how to do it."

Olivia's face contorted with pain. "Me either."

The next minute they were hugging each other, tears streaming down both their faces. Olivia literally felt as if her heart were breaking.

She knew they were doing the right thing, that they had reached the point where they couldn't make things work anymore. But she also knew it was going to be unbearable to lose Roger. How was she ever going to make it through the rest of the week, the rest of the year?

Four

"I've decided what to do for the photographic essay," Jeffrey told Elizabeth on Thursday morning. They had gotten to school early and were sitting at a table in the student lounge, sharing a carton of orange juice.

"Really? What?" Elizabeth asked with interest.

"Well, it's going to be a mood piece, set down at the beach and out by the canyon. It's going to be a series of pictures of a girl, most of them kind of filmy. All black-and-white. The point is to show this girl in a state of transition. In the first photos she'll look very dreamy and sad, and then gradually more sure of herself. The last one will be partly shaded, with a suggestion that she's really happy."

43

"That sounds neat," Elizabeth said. "Who are you going to use as a model?"

"Well, actually, I've been thinking about that a lot. I kind of assumed I was going to ask *you*." Jeffrey frowned. "But your face is far too sunny, too happy, for the early shots to work. I don't know. . . ." He looked up at her. "I was thinking Olivia might be good. What do you think?"

"Olivia?" Elizabeth repeated. She was thoughtful for a moment. "Yes," she agreed. "Olivia has the right face—the kind of face that shows what she's feeling inside. I think she'd be really good."

Jeffrey nodded. "Yes, and besides, I think it would help her to have something extra to do to keep busy. I had to call her last night, and she told me that she and Roger have broken up for good. I think she's feeling pretty miserable."

Elizabeth set down the carton of juice. "Oh, no," she said softly. "Jeffrey, I was positive they'd be able to work things out! Did she give you any idea why it happened?"

Jeffrey shook his head. "Not really. She said something about the fact that they had been arguing a lot, that they basically seem to want different things and just can't really be good to each other—or for each other—anymore."

Poor Olivia, Elizabeth thought with a pang. The girl was so sensitive, so accustomed to Roger's support. It was going to be very hard for her to get used to being without him.

"I think it's a terrific idea. And I think Olivia is lucky to have a friend like you," Elizabeth said seriously. She felt a shiver inside. Poor Roger and Olivia. If they could break up, anyone could. But she and Jeffrey were different, she assured herself. And they certainly weren't having any problems. Everything was great between them. "She's a wonderful choice for the photo essay. She's so pretty."

"Do you think so?" Jeffrey asked curiously. "I actually wouldn't call her *pretty*. But there's something haunting about her face . . . something very interesting. Photographers are always looking for faces like that."

Elizabeth finished the juice with a slurp. "It's going to be great," she said.

Jeffrey smiled at her. "You know something? I love you." He leaned over and kissed her cheek. "You always make me think my crazy ideas are good."

Elizabeth giggled. "I happen to be one of your crazy ideas, don't I?" She kissed him back, the shivery feeling evaporating.

Nothing could ever come between Jeffrey and her. She was sure of it!

*   *   *

45

"Hey," Jessica said, opening her slam book to the section marked Crystal Ball and unfolding the pages. "Look what someone wrote in my book under Couple of the Future." She showed the notebook to her sister.

Elizabeth stared at the entry. Sure enough, right there in neat blue ink, it said, "Olivia Davidson and Jeffrey French"!

"That's ridiculous," Elizabeth said. "That's obviously somebody's idea of a stupid joke."

Lila crowded over for a look. "Olivia and Jeffrey? That's a dumb combination. Olivia's with Roger."

"They broke up," Jessica said, studying the entry with interest. "Does anyone recognize this writing? I wonder who could have written it."

Elizabeth tried hard to seem unconcerned. "Someone silly. Let's just forget it, Jess."

Jessica lifted her brows. "You mean you're not upset? Boy, I'd be furious." She held the notebook closer, squinting at the blue ink. "Maybe Olivia wrote it," she mused. "Do you think she's after Jeffrey, Liz? Now that she's on the rebound and everything?"

"Of course she isn't," Elizabeth scoffed. She couldn't believe how ridiculous her sister could be sometimes. "They're friends, that's all. And they're spending a lot of time together lately because Jeffrey's helping Olivia with the literary magazine she's starting up. That's all there is to it."

"Hmm," Jessica said thoughtfully. "Well, if it were me, I'd be totally freaking out about it. But I'm probably too sensitive about stuff like that. See, you're so *unsuspecting*, Liz. It would never even occur to you that Olivia might be trying to steal Jeffrey away from you."

Elizabeth tried to concentrate on her lunch, but she seemed to have lost her appetite. "Look," she said, "why would Olivia be after Jeffrey? She just broke up with Roger *yesterday*, for heaven's sake. The last thing she's going to want is to get involved right away again."

Jessica rolled her eyes. "Please," she moaned. "Liz, how can my very own sister be so hopefully naive? *Of course* she's going to want another boyfriend right away! She's lonely and heartbroken, and I bet Jeffrey is exactly the kind of guy who can soothe her, be a real shoulder for her to cry on. And all the while she'll be worming her way in deeper and deeper—"

"I don't think so, Jess," Lila objected. "You're making it sound like the poor girl's been scheming for ages. Liz says she and Roger just broke up yesterday."

Elizabeth nodded. "Lila's right, Jess. Olivia hasn't even had time to realize what's happened yet."

47

Jessica sniffed. "Well," she said, "I never trusted that girl." In fact, a long time ago, when it first came out that Roger was the long-lost nephew of Bruce Patman's father, Jessica herself had tried her darnedest to steal him away from Olivia. It hadn't worked, and ever since then she had held a grudge.

"When did she ask Jeffrey to edit this magazine with her?" she demanded.

Elizabeth frowned, trying to remember. "Just recently. But Jeffrey said no," she added.

"Right. He's just spending about as much time helping out as he would've spent co-editing, isn't he?" Jessica asked.

Elizabeth's brow was furrowed. Jessica was really starting to get her upset.

"Jessica," she said, "I would really appreciate it if you'd stop talking nonsense. Olivia happens to be a friend of mine, OK? There's no way in the world she'd try to steal Jeffrey away. They're working together, and that's all there is to it."

Jessica rolled her eyes. "Oh, Liz, you're *so* trusting," she moaned.

"You make it sound as though I'm stupid," Elizabeth snapped. "I happen to believe that trust is what makes a relationship work, OK? So just quit giving me that pitying look of yours."

All the same, she couldn't help thinking about

Jeffrey's decision to use Olivia in his photo essay. She was glad Jessica didn't know about that yet.

She didn't feel like having to defend Jeffrey right now. And she was really glad when Cara came over to join them and the conversation turned to the basketball game the next night in the gym.

For the moment Elizabeth wanted to forget all about the incriminating entry in the slam book.

A big group of girls from the junior class was congregating out on the lawn after school, soaking up the California sunshine and reading aloud from their slam books. Elizabeth and Enid Rollins were on their way out to the parking lot when Lila waved them over.

"Come hear some of these entries! They're hysterical!" she urged.

Enid, Elizabeth's dearest friend, had already remarked privately that she thought the slam books were getting out of hand. Enid was an incredibly loyal and sensitive girl, and like Elizabeth, she didn't want to see people get hurt. "Let's go ahead," she murmured to Elizabeth. The two girls were on their way to Enid's house to study together.

"No, let's stay for a few minutes," Elizabeth said. Jeffrey was photographing Olivia that afternoon, and Elizabeth felt like taking her mind off her own worries. Listening to slam book entries seemed like a good way.

"Most Likely to Earn a Million Dollars Before Thirty—Bruce Patman," Lila read from her book.

"*Earn* it," Amy said sarcastically. "That'll be the day."

"Most Artistic—Olivia Davidson," Cara read from her book.

"Best Legs—Aaron Dallas."

"Most All-Around Nice—Elizabeth Wakefield," Maria Santelli read.

"I have Enid Rollins for the same entry," DeeDee Gordon chimed in.

"Most Likely to Have Six Kids—Jessica Wakefield!" Everyone cracked up at that, and Jessica pretended to look hurt.

"I get all the great ones," she complained. "First I'm the biggest flirt, and now I'm the most likely to have a billion babies."

"The Crystal Ball ones are the best," Lila said. "Amy, what do you have under future predictions?"

Amy smiled. "Winston Egbert as Most Likely to Run for President." Then she frowned. "This is strange. Someone must be starting a bad rumor, Liz."

"Why?" Elizabeth asked, trying not to look concerned.

"Because it says Olivia and Jeffrey under Couple of the Future in my book."

"In mine, too!" Cara exclaimed.

"Mine, too," DeeDee Gordon said.

Everyone looked at Elizabeth, who didn't have the faintest idea what to say or do. "Oh, well," she said with a forced smile. "You know what predictions are like. Not very likely to come true, right?"

Everyone kept looking at her, and Elizabeth felt increasingly uncomfortable.

"Come on, you guys," Enid said suddenly. "What do you want Liz to say? Whoever's writing these entries is a real jerk and just trying to start trouble." She turned back to Elizabeth and patted her reassuringly on the shoulder. "Can we get going *now*?" she pleaded.

Elizabeth nodded dully. Who in the world would be writing a thing like that in people's slam books?

One thing was for certain. She intended to talk to Jeffrey about it and make sure he was as bothered by it as she was. Until then she wasn't going to be able to put it out of her mind.

Five

Jessica took extra-long getting ready for the basketball game on Friday night. She scrutinized her reflection for ages in the bathroom mirror, swirling around in her red-and-white cheerleading outfit to see how she looked in action. Tonight was the first time A.J. was going to see her cheer, and she wanted to look her best. When she got to school, she spent another ten minutes in the locker room brushing her hair.

"Come on, Jess. This is a basketball game, not a debutante ball," Robin Wilson teased her. Robin was the other co-captain and split responsibility with Jessica for the team.

"Who is it, Jess?" Maria Santelli demanded.

"Yeah," Sandra Bacon said, brushing a piece

of lint off her skirt. "It must mean a guy is involved if Jessica's glued to the mirror like this!"

Jean West giggled. "Out with it, Jess. We know you're interested in *someone*. Who is it?"

Ordinarily Jessica would have flipped back her hair and given the girls a smart answer. But to her dismay she actually blushed and started to stammer when she tried to answer.

"I—uh, well—uh . . ."

Robin glanced at her watch. "Come on, you guys. We've got to get out there and start cheering. We'll have to wait until halftime to find out who's Jessica's heartthrob."

Soon the cheerleaders were out in the brightly lit gymnasium, lining up in the configuration for their first cheer. Jessica was craning her neck, trying to see the basketball players when they came out. She was so busy trying to locate A.J. that she missed her cue. The rest of the line jumped in unison, and Jessica, half a beat off, stuck out like a jack-in-the-box.

Robin frowned. "Let's start over," she hissed.

They started over, this time in unison. But just then the whistle blew, and the players rushed out in their shorts and mesh shirts. Jessica stared at A.J., her heart pounding, and absolutely froze. She barely noticed that the other cheerleaders were forming rows for the pyramid.

"Jessica!" Maria hissed, nudging her.

"Oh!" Jessica gasped, turning beet red. The players had huddled around the coach in front of the bleachers, and she was still so intent on A.J. that she couldn't seem to get anything right. The pyramid was ruined because of her. And the first two cheers went badly, too.

"Jessica, what on earth is wrong with you tonight?" Robin demanded in a low voice.

"I—uh, I really don't know, Robin. I'm just really uncoordinated for some reason."

"Why don't you quit staring at the basketball players?" Maria suggested. Everyone laughed, and Jessica felt like an idiot.

"OK," she said, drawing herself up with an effort. "I'm fine now." It took everything she had in her not to turn and stare at A.J., but Jessica forced herself to concentrate. And for the rest of the first quarter she managed to keep in time with the others and not draw attention to herself. In fact, she was finally beginning to relax, thinking the night was going to be OK— Sweet Valley was ahead twenty-eight to sixteen, and everyone was having a great time— when A.J. came up to the basket to shoot.

"A.J.! A.J.!" everyone cheered.

A.J. jumped up, looking so graceful and handsome, Jessica couldn't believe it. He shot well, but the ball hit the rim of the basket and bounced backward, right toward the cheerleaders.

"Get it, Jess," Robin said as it rolled directly toward her.

Jessica stared at the ball, then up at A.J., who was coming toward her to retrieve it. She leaned over to scoop it up and took a tentative step or two toward the redhead, thinking all the while, *What if I touch his hand.* . . . She couldn't believe she was acting this way. But her heart was absolutely pounding the whole time she looked at him.

"Jessica, you should see the color of your face. It's as red as an apple," Maria said with a giggle when Jessica had returned the ball and come back to join the others.

"*I* think Jessica has a crush on A.J.," Sandra Bacon declared.

Jean smiled. "I think so, too," she agreed.

Amy Sutton could hardly believe her ears. "Jess? In love with A.J.?"

"I am not," Jessica said hotly. "Leave me alone, you guys." Feeling confused and angry, she stomped over to one of the bleachers to sit down.

"Boy, what's wrong with her?" she could hear Amy demanding.

Jessica felt her eyes fill with tears. What *was*

wrong with her? All she knew was that she didn't want to be teased about A.J. Couldn't her friends understand that this was *serious?*

"You seem quiet," Jeffrey murmured to Elizabeth. "What's the matter? Is anything wrong?"

They were sitting together on the top row of the bleachers, watching Sweet Valley demolish Riverside High. The score in the third quarter was 78 to 46, and the crowd on the Sweet Valley side was going wild. Elizabeth knew that she *was* being pretty quiet and that she must seem all the more subdued in contrast to the wild cheering around them.

The truth was, she had felt tense all evening. She'd been absolutely determined not to let those silly slam book entries get to her, but finally she couldn't stand it anymore.

"This is going to sound dumb," she said to Jeffrey now, "but in some of the slam books someone's been predicting that you and Olivia are going to be a future couple."

Jeffrey frowned. "What? I don't get it."

Elizabeth had to explain to him how the Crystal Ball category in the slam books worked. Gradually an expression of comprehension broke over his face.

"I get it. And someone wrote that Olivia and I—"

"More than *someone*," Elizabeth interrupted. "It must be written in about a dozen books by now."

Jeffrey laughed, put his arm around her, and gave her a hug. "Don't get mad at me for saying so, Liz, but I can't believe you'd get upset about something like that. You know what people are like. They could say anything!"

Elizabeth bit her lip. "But why would anyone think that about you and Olivia?" she protested.

Jeffrey didn't seem disturbed. "I don't know why. People think whatever they want to think. Maybe because she and I have been spending so much time together working on the literary magazine. But you know better than to believe something like that, Liz." Jeffrey stared at her. "Don't you?"

Elizabeth swallowed hard. Rationally she knew it was crazy to be jealous. Jeffrey couldn't start to care for another girl as long as he loved her. And theirs was an open, honest relationship. She would know if anything was wrong.

But deep down she felt insecure. She wanted Jeffrey to reassure her, to kiss her and tell her that he loved her more than anything in the world. Instead, Jeffrey was acting sensible. Everything he said was *right*, but it didn't really help to make her feel better.

"Just to show you what a nut you are," Jeffrey continued, "I asked Olivia to join us tonight at the game." He looked at his watch. "But I guess she decided she couldn't make it. Now, is there any way I'd ask her to come join us if I secretly liked her?"

Elizabeth thought about this. "No," she said faintly. "I guess not."

"Maybe we'll see her at the Dairi Burger. A whole bunch of people are meeting there after the game," Jeffrey added.

Elizabeth frowned. The truth was, she had wanted to spend some time alone with Jeffrey after the game. They had seen so little of each other lately, and she had hoped they might take off alone later, instead of joining the crowd, maybe drive somewhere romantic and have a nice long talk. And instead . . .

Just then A.J. scored another basket, and everyone in the bleachers jumped up to applaud and shout his name. Jeffrey rose with everyone else, cheering.

Elizabeth sighed and stood up to cheer. This clearly wasn't the moment for a heart-to-heart talk with Jeffrey. She would just have to wait until they had a chance to be alone.

* * *

"Let's go over there," Jeffrey said, squeezing Elizabeth's hand. They were pushing their way through the crowd inside the Dairi Burger, trying to find some place to sit. Olivia Davidson was nowhere in sight, but it looked as though most of the spectators from the game had poured inside the popular hamburger joint. Jeffrey led Elizabeth to a corner booth, where Jessica, Amy, Aaron Dallas, and Ken Matthews were sitting. Jeffrey and Elizabeth approached the booth at the same time as A.J.

"Is there room here for one more?" A.J. asked, after Jeffrey and Elizabeth slid in.

"Sure. We'll make room," Aaron said. "Anyone who scores twenty-eight points in one night can sit in my booth!"

Everyone laughed, and Ken slapped A.J. on the back.

"I'm going to make a new entry in my slam book," Amy said, taking it out of her backpack. "Highest Scorer—A. J. Morgan."

Everyone laughed again, and Ken looked curiously at Amy's notebook. "Those things are all over the place lately. What have I gotten called?"

"Hmm, let's see. Biggest Jock," Amy told him.

"Not bad," Ken said, sounding pleased.

"We had slam books at my old school in

Atlanta," A.J. said. "I always got put in categories like Reddest Head. Not very exciting."

Jessica squirmed. She hoped no one turned to Biggest Flirt.

To her dismay A.J. had picked up Robin's slam book and started flipping through it. "Best Looking . . . Smartest . . . Best Couple . . . Biggest Flirt," he read aloud. Jessica held her breath.

"Biggest Flirt," A.J. repeated. His eyes ran down the page. Jessica felt her stomach doing flip-flops. "Wow," he said. "Ten votes for Jessica Wakefield." Everyone at the table laughed, except for Jessica, who felt her cheeks burning. A.J. looked at her curiously. "That sure doesn't seem right to me," he said warmly, staring straight into her eyes.

That made everything all right again, and Jessica didn't even hear what Aaron said in response. She kept her eyes lowered, her face averted. She couldn't believe how happy it made her feel to hear him say that. Did that mean he liked her? God, she hoped so!

She knew no one in the world would believe it, but she was in love. Really, totally, in love. She was so much in love that she felt like a new person, and all she wanted to think about was A.J.

"Hey, look at this," Aaron said, taking the slam book from A.J. and flipping ahead to the

Crystal Ball category. "Future Couples . . . Olivia Davidson and Jeffrey French."

"Oooh," Ken Matthews moaned. "Watch out, Liz!"

Everyone laughed. Everyone, that is, but Elizabeth.

"And look what's right under it! Elizabeth Wakefield—and A. J. Morgan!"

This exclamation was greeted with surprised silence. Everyone looked nervously from Elizabeth to A.J. to see what their responses would be.

"That's pretty flattering," A.J. said with a grin, and the tension broke. Everyone laughed again, including Elizabeth.

Everyone but Jeffrey—and Jessica, who stared at her sister with a look of horror in her eyes.

Six

Elizabeth knocked on her sister's door early Saturday morning. She was in good spirits again. It was a gorgeous day, and she and Jeffrey had plans to go to the beach later on that afternoon. Her concerns from the night before had faded and, in fact, she was beginning to berate herself for having acted so irrationally about Olivia. The poor girl was naturally feeling lonesome now that she and Roger had split up. Luckily she had the literary magazine to work on to help keep her mind off her sorrows and luckily, too, Jeffrey—nice guy that he was—was around to give Olivia the support she needed. Elizabeth felt slightly ashamed now that she had let the slam book entries bother her.

"Who is it?" Jessica called in a groggy voice.

"It's me. Can I come in?"

Silence followed. After a minute Jessica said grumpily, "Go away. I want to sleep, Liz."

Elizabeth thought it over, shrugged, and headed downstairs to the sun-filled Spanish-tiled kitchen where Mrs. Wakefield was finishing a cup of coffee and reading the morning paper.

"Hi," Elizabeth said, slipping into the chair across from her. Her mother looked great in her light blue jogging suit. She could easily pass for the twins' older sister with her blond pageboy, sparkling blue eyes, and flawless skin.

"Hi, honey. Did you sleep well? How was the game?"

Elizabeth poured herself some cereal. "Pretty fun." She studied her mother closely for a minute. "Mom? Have you ever gotten . . . I know this is going to sound kind of dumb, but have you ever gotten jealous of, well, you know, some other woman?"

Mrs. Wakefield laughed. "Your father and I have known each other for a long time, honey. You know how we both feel about that. If a couple can't trust each other, there's bound to be trouble."

"I know." Elizabeth frowned. "But haven't you *ever* gotten jealous? Even a teeny little bit?"

Mrs. Wakefield was thoughtful for a moment. "You know, come to think of it . . . when your father first started working for the law firm where he is now, there was a young attorney named Annabel. A British woman, very pretty, very smart—and I think very interested in Dad," Mrs. Wakefield mused. "I wasn't exactly *jealous*, but I can distinctly remember feeling uncomfortable at the thought of her pursuing him." She smiled. "I'd forgotten all about that, but, yes, I suppose I *was* a little bit jealous."

Elizabeth thought this over. "So it doesn't necessarily mean you don't really love someone if you get, you know, kind of jealous."

"Heavens, no!" Mrs. Wakefield exclaimed. "It seems to me it's one of the most natural feelings in the world. Though I *do* think it's a feeling worth fighting. I think trusting the person you love is the best thing you can possibly do." She looked closely at Elizabeth. "Why do you ask, sweetheart? Are you worried about Jeffrey?"

Elizabeth was about to answer when Jessica came stomping into the kitchen, still in her pajamas, her hair sticking out all over the place.

"Liz," she said accusingly, her eyes flashing, "did you take one of my headbands from my top drawer?"

Elizabeth stared at her. Jessica sounded unbelievably angry. "I guess I borrowed one a few days ago," she said.

"Well, give it back," Jessica snapped.

"Jess," Elizabeth protested, "how many times have you borrowed something from me without asking? It was just that I was going jogging and couldn't find one of my own, and I thought— "

"Give it back," Jessica repeated angrily.

"Jessica," Mrs. Wakefield said mildly, "I think your sister has a point. And in any case, I don't think you should be using that tone of voice."

"Liz," Jessica said in a tone of aggrieved control, "could you possibly come upstairs with me and help me find my headband?"

Elizabeth gave her mother a puzzled look and got to her feet.

Jessica was obviously furious about something. And Elizabeth didn't think it was the headband that was bothering her, either!

"What's the matter with you?" Elizabeth demanded once they got upstairs.

Jessica's eyes were flashing with anger. "I told you. I don't like you rummaging around in my drawers, that's all."

"Jessica—" Elizabeth began.

But Jessica cut her off. "And another thing. I don't like the way you were acting last night at the Dairi Burger." She crossed her arms, glaring at her twin. "Don't you think you were being pretty obvious?"

Elizabeth was getting more and more confused. "What do you mean? Pretty obvious about what?"

"You know. The way you were just using A.J. to get back at Jeffrey. I mean, *I* know how mad you are because Jeffrey's spending all his time with Olivia. But I don't see what good it's going to do to flirt with A.J."

Elizabeth stared at her, her eyes wide with astonishment. "Me? Flirting with A.J.?"

"Yeah, you," Jessica snapped. "Flirting with A.J. Come on, Liz. Don't give me that innocent look. You know as well as I do that's what you were doing."

Elizabeth couldn't believe her ears. "I wasn't flirting with him," she cried. "Jessica, you're out of your mind! I barely said one thing to him! In fact, I think all I did was smile!" She knew she sounded defensive, but she felt Jessica's accusation was coming out of nowhere. "What was I supposed to do, sit across from the guy and not even smile at him when he smiled at me?"

"Fine," Jessica said. "If that's how you want to be about it, that's just fine, Liz. All I'm saying is that I don't like it."

Elizabeth stared at her sister. "Listen, Jess. Are you interested in this guy?"

"No!" Jessica shouted, then lowered her voice. "I'm not. I just don't like seeing my very own twin acting like a—like—" Her eyes filled with tears.

Elizabeth shook her head, completely baffled. "Jessica, I don't know what to say. I'm sorry if I upset you somehow. But I certainly wasn't flirting with A.J." She was thoughtful for a moment. "You're not upset because of that stupid entry in Robin's slam book, are you?"

"Why should I be? I told you, I couldn't care less about A. J. Morgan," Jessica shot back.

"Then why—" Elizabeth broke off. "OK, OK," she said, relenting when she saw the stormy look in her sister's eyes. "Clearly this is beyond me, Jess."

The telephone rang, and the twins looked at each other. "It's probably Jeffrey," Elizabeth said just as Jessica said, "That must be Lila."

It rang again, and Jessica lunged for it.

"Oh," she said, disappointed, "it's for you," and she handed Elizabeth the receiver. "It's Jeffrey."

Elizabeth took the phone in silence. She couldn't for the life of her understand why her sister was behaving the way she was. Was she telling the truth about A.J.? It was bizarre, but on the other hand Elizabeth couldn't think of a single time in her twin's whole life when she had liked a guy and not admitted it. So obviously *that* wasn't what was bothering her. At any rate, it didn't look as if Elizabeth were going to find out the real reason for her irritation. At least not right then.

"Liz?" Jeffrey sounded far away, and the connection was slightly fuzzy. She could hear traffic behind him. "Liz, it's Jeffrey."

"Where are you? You sound like you're on Mars." She giggled.

"Actually, pretty close to it. I'm at a rest stop off Route Nine. Olivia's with me—we're heading out to Las Palmas Canyon to do a part of this photo essay."

Elizabeth bit her lip. "Oh," she said. She glanced down at her watch. "What about going to the beach?"

"Well, I'm—just a second, Liz." He covered the receiver, and she could hear a faint buzzing for a second. "Listen," he resumed. "I'm going to be a little later than I thought. Liv and I were going to do this tomorrow, but when I woke up and saw the light, I realized today would be better. It's the perfect light for taking pictures, Liz."

Liv? Elizabeth couldn't help thinking. Since when did he call Olivia *Liv*? "What time do you think you'll be back?" she asked, trying to restrain herself. *Remember what Mom said*, she instructed herself. *Trust him.*

"Well, we should be back by two. Is that OK? I promise to work as fast as I can. And we can still go to the beach when I get back."

"OK, Jeffrey. That sounds fine." Elizabeth was proud of the way she sounded—controlled, mature, trusting. "Tell Olivia I said hello."

"Mmm—OK. See you soon."

"Jeffrey?" Suddenly a terrible wave of insecurity washed over her. "I love you."

"Me, too." Jeffrey sounded brisk, almost businesslike. "I'll see you later, Liz." And the next thing she heard was the click as he hung up the phone.

By two-fifteen Elizabeth was starting to lose her patience. She was all ready for the beach. She had her new striped bikini on under her shorts and T-shirt, and her beach bag was all packed. But Jeffrey was nowhere to be seen.

The door bell rang, and Elizabeth raced to the front door. "Oh, Cara," she said, her face falling. Not that she wasn't pleased to see the pretty brunette. She liked Cara more and more now that she was dating Steven. But she had been hoping it would be Jeffrey.

Cara looked distinctly uncomfortable. "I've come to pick up Jessica. We're heading for the beach," Cara said, avoiding Elizabeth's gaze as she came into the foyer. "How are you, Liz?" Her voice sounded forced, artificial.

"OK. Actually, I'm . . . maybe I should come with you guys. I'm waiting for Jeffrey, but he seems to be taking forever."

Cara fiddled nervously with her bracelet. "Liz," she said, "can I ask you something? And you have to promise to be totally honest. If you'd seen something . . . like, say you'd seen Steven with another girl, and you knew I didn't know about it. Would you tell me?" Her nervousness seemed to be increasing.

"It depends." Elizabeth thought it over. "I might not want to interfere. Especially since we're talking about my brother. But—well, I don't know." She stared at the brunette. "Why? You aren't trying to tell me something, are you?"

Cara looked miserable. "It's just that it makes me so angry! You're one of the sweetest people I know, Liz. And I can't stand the thought of anyone hurting you."

"Who—" Elizabeth frowned. "Cara, I know you're trying to tell me something. Is it about Jeffrey?"

Cara nodded. "I had a dentist appointment this morning in Riverside. I was driving back and I had to stop, so I turned into the rest area on Route Nine. And I saw Jeffrey's car." She was really upset. "Well, I figured I'd go over and say hi. Then I saw he wasn't alone. I thought it was you he was with, so I kept walking toward the car." She bit her lip. "It was Olivia, though. Not you. And he had his arms around her!"

Elizabeth felt the color drain from her face. "Are you sure?" she asked faintly.

Cara nodded. "You know I wouldn't say anything otherwise. No, it was definitely them. And they were definitely holding each other."

Elizabeth took a deep breath. *Don't jump to conclusions*, she told herself. *Maybe there's a perfectly rational explanation for this.*

But then her anger got the better of her, and she couldn't stand it anymore. Suddenly everything seemed to add up: Jeffrey spending so much time working on the magazine; Jeffrey choosing Olivia to be his model for the photo essay; Olivia and Roger breaking up. Elizabeth was sick and tired of defending Jeffrey, trying to make up excuses for him. What explanation could there possibly be? Jeffrey was in love with Olivia, that was all there was to it. And she wasn't going to sit here and wait for him to come over and tell her so himself. No way.

"Cara, I'm going to come with you guys to the beach if that's OK," Elizabeth said. "I—well, to be honest, I don't really feel like being alone right now."

Cara gave her a sympathetic hug. "I don't blame you. Just stay right here, and I'll run upstairs and get your sister."

Elizabeth felt hot tears spill down her cheeks. She couldn't believe it. How could Jeffrey do something like this to her? The thought of him holding Olivia . . . kissing her . . . made her completely sick.

She felt like such a fool, trying to convince herself to trust Jeffrey when all the signals had pointed to this.

Well, Elizabeth wasn't going to let herself be stepped on. She loved Jeffrey, but if it was over, it was over. And she wasn't going to beg him to come back. In fact, quite the opposite! Elizabeth pulled herself up to her full height. She wasn't going to let anyone know that her heart was breaking. Not Jeffrey, not anyone.

And she certainly wasn't going to sit at home and mope!

Seven

By two-thirty, when Jessica, Elizabeth, and Cara showed up at the beach, dozens of their friends and classmates were out enjoying the warm afternoon sun. A volleyball game was going on at one end of the beach. Radios were blaring, and the line outside the Snack Shack was long—typical for Sweet Valley on a Saturday. Surfers were busy trying out the waves, and a few brave windsurfers tried their luck in the more sheltered cove. It was an absolutely perfect afternoon, perfect in every way but one, Elizabeth thought.

"There's Lila," Jessica said, pointing to a massive terry towel several yards from the lifeguard's stand. The towel said THE RITZ in big letters, and right at the end of the writing sat Lila in a shiny gold bathing suit.

"Where on earth did she get that suit?" Cara muttered.

Elizabeth couldn't believe it either. Her own striped bikini seemed plain by comparison.

"Daddy got it for me," Lila explained when Jessica and Cara demanded to know where the suit came from. "From Milan. Italy's the *best*," she added complacently, digging around in her beach bag for some suntan oil. "You guys should try to get some stuff airmailed over for you. Sweet Valley just doesn't have any real *selection*."

"Yeah, well, we do what we can," Jessica said sarcastically.

Lila smoothed expensive oil over her long legs. "I've been dying for you guys to get here. It's been totally dead all day."

Cara laughed. "Looks pretty lively to me," she said.

Lila shrugged. "No one *interesting* is here." She patted the sand beside her. "Come on, put your towels down. I need some company."

Elizabeth concentrated hard on unfolding her towel. She didn't feel like making conversation and hoped they'd all let her soak up some sun in peace. But luck wasn't on her side.

"Where's Jeffrey, Liz?" Lila asked brightly.

Elizabeth groaned.

"Bad question, Li," Jessica said softly.

"Really? What have I missed? Don't tell me the Best Couple is having a lovers' spat," Lila said.

Elizabeth frowned. "Not a lovers' spat. Let's just say a parting of the ways."

"What are you talking about?" Lila shrieked. "You and Jeffrey are perfect for each other! You can't be serious, Liz. I don't believe it."

Elizabeth's eyes filled with tears. "I thought we were perfect for each other, too. But it turns out I was wrong. It seems that Jeffrey and Olivia have kind of—" it broke Elizabeth's heart just to say it out loud—"fallen for each other. That's why they've been spending so much time together."

"I don't believe it. Olivia? You've got to be kidding," Lila said, her eyes opened wide in astonishment.

"I'm not kidding," Elizabeth said flatly. "I thought it was dumb when I first saw it in one of those slam books. But it turns out to be true. I can hardly act like nothing's wrong. He's been spending every waking second with her!"

Lila frowned. "Wait a minute. Let me make sure I've got this straight. You think Jeffrey's in love with Olivia Davidson. Right?"

"Right." Elizabeth swallowed hard.

"What does Jeffrey say about it? Have you two talked about this?"

"I—" Elizabeth stared at her. "No, of course not! I can hardly sit down and say, 'OK, Jeffrey, tell me why Cara happened to see you with your arms around Olivia today.'"

Lila's eyes bulged. "You saw them?" she demanded, turning to Cara.

Cara nodded.

"Wow." Lila was quiet for a minute. "Liz, that's bad, I admit it. But it's still no reason to panic. You've absolutely *got* to talk it over with him. Tell him that you trust him and love him and all that, but you need to ask him a few teeny little questions about what's been going on between Olivia and him. Don't let him know you're jealous. It never works if you do."

Elizabeth shook her head. "Forget it, Lila. I've already decided it isn't worth it. I don't want to put Jeffrey on the spot, and I certainly don't want to start pleading with him for excuses or explanations or anything. If he's in love with Olivia—" She had to gulp back the tears. "If he's in love with Olivia, fine. That's it. It's all over between us." She squinted at the water, trying to keep the tears from pouring down her cheeks.

"Well," Lila said philosophically, "I guess if that's the way you feel. . . ."

"That *is* the way I feel," Elizabeth said fiercely. "And I don't want to talk about it anymore."

Lila leaned forward suddenly and put her hand on Elizabeth's arm. "Maybe if *I* talked to him," she said. "You know, just to kind of see how he's really feeling."

Elizabeth kept staring straight in front of her. "Go ahead," she said flatly. "But you won't be able to find him. He isn't here. He's off somewhere with *her*."

Lila didn't say anything. And as far as Elizabeth was concerned, that was it. The conversation was over.

"Hey," Cara said, sitting forward. "Is that A.J. over there with Ken and Aaron? He looks cute in a bathing suit."

Jessica sat up straight, her eyes very wide. "Where?" she demanded anxiously, staring straight at A.J.

Elizabeth was looking in the same direction, a little smile playing on her lips. "He really is kind of cute, isn't he?" she mused. She was remembering what happened the night before when Robin had read that silly prediction in the Crystal Ball section of her slam book—that one day A.J. and Elizabeth would be a couple. Come to think of it, it *was* kind of flattering. He seemed like such a nice guy—so easygoing, so friendly, and *definitely* cute. He wasn't really her type, but what harm could there possibly be in having a little fun flirting with him? At the very least it would take her mind off Jeffrey and Olivia.

"You know," she said, turning to her sister, "you gave me a good idea about last night. I wasn't trying to flirt with A.J. then. But maybe I should. Maybe it would make me feel better about Jeffrey and Olivia."

"Flirt with *who*?" Jessica squeaked out, her face ashen.

"With A. J. Morgan," Elizabeth said silkily, getting to her feet in one smooth motion.

"Liz!" Jessica shrieked. "You can't do that!"

"Well . . ." Elizabeth frowned. "I know it isn't really me. And I'll probably botch it up. But I can't just go around moping about Jeffrey all day. I've got to do something. Maybe flirting with A.J. is the way to go!"

Jessica's mouth dropped open, but she didn't say a word. She watched her twin walk across the sand to where the boys were standing.

A.J. was heading over to the volleyball game with Ken and Aaron when Elizabeth stopped him.

"A.J.," she purred, staring up at him from

under her lashes, "weren't you even going to come over and say hi?"

Aaron and Ken exchanged confused glances. "Jess?" Aaron asked.

"It's Liz, silly," Elizabeth said lightly. She didn't care what they thought. In fact, she was enjoying herself. It felt good to act so completely, totally out of character. For once she wasn't being serious, dependable, earnest Elizabeth Wakefield—Jeffrey's girlfriend. Or ex-girlfriend. She was doing exactly as she pleased!

A.J. looked every bit as confused as Aaron and Ken, if not more so. "Should I have come over? I was just, uh, we were just—"

"The minute you got here I started wondering," Elizabeth interrupted, putting her hand on his arm, "if you'd come say hi or if you were going to act like a total stranger. After all, A.J., you and I have something in common."

"What's that?" he asked, his brow wrinkling.

Elizabeth tucked her arm through his. "You know," she said significantly.

"No, I don't. What?" he asked again.

"We got matched up in Robin's slam book. Isn't that enough of a bond to warrant a hello?" Elizabeth asked coyly.

Aaron and Ken were staring at each other now with frank amazement and dismay.

"A.J.," she said impulsively, ignoring the

glances of the others, "come and buy me a hot dog. I'm absolutely starving."

A.J. looked questioningly at his two new friends.

"Go ahead," Aaron said. "We're not going anywhere."

A.J. gulped. "Well, uh, sure, Liz." He gave her a weak smile, and Elizabeth, her arm still tucked through his, gave him a huge smile back.

Not that she really felt much like smiling. But she had sworn she was going to hide what she was really feeling. And so far she had to admit she was doing a pretty good job!

Jessica, watching A.J. and Elizabeth wander off toward the Snack Shack, was fuming.

"Looks like she did it!" Lila said with a tone of glee.

Jessica stared in stony silence after her twin. She couldn't remember when she had been this mad at Elizabeth. How could her sister do something like this to her?

The truth was that the minute Jessica saw A.J., her heart began pounding wildly and her palms started sweating. No guy had ever, for as long as she could remember, had such an effect on her. True, she had had plenty of crushes before. And once or twice she had even thought she might be falling in love. But it didn't feel like this. She had never felt this before—this overwhelming sense that nothing else mattered when A.J. was around. In spite of her awkwardness in front of him, she longed to spend some time alone with him, let him know what she was really like. She spent hours daydreaming about what it would feel like to be in his arms, to touch his soft red curls.

And now Elizabeth was purposely going off to flirt with him, just to spite Jeffrey! Jessica didn't think she could stand it. The blinding jealousy that came over her was so intense, she thought she might explode.

She told herself she should just run after Elizabeth and tell her how she felt. But she couldn't. She couldn't say a word.

"Jess, what's wrong?" Lila demanded. "You look a little sick. Are you getting too much sun or something?"

"I'm fine," Jessica said shortly. She was staring at Elizabeth and A.J., unable to wrench her gaze away.

"I think they make kind of a cute couple," Cara said thoughtfully. "I'm glad Liz is giving Jeffrey a taste of his own medicine!"

Jessica squirmed miserably. This was unbearable for her. "Do you think A.J. likes my sister?" she asked, trying to keep her voice nonchalant.

"Who wouldn't?" Lila interposed. "Liz is a great girl. Pretty, smart, funny. What guy in his right mind wouldn't be thrilled to find out she's interested in him?"

Jessica stared hopelessly down the beach after them. All she knew was that if Elizabeth really did break up with Jeffrey and started going out with A.J., she would never talk to Elizabeth again.

Eight

"Uh-oh," Lila said, shading her eyes with her hand. "Here come Jeffrey and Olivia. I have a bad feeling about this, guys."

Jessica, Cara, and Lila were still perched on their towels in the center of the action near the lifeguard's chair when they saw Jeffrey and Olivia crossing down from the farthest parking lot. Jeffrey was wearing jeans and a T-shirt, and Olivia was wearing a sundress and carrying her sandals. They both appeared distracted and worried and were looking around them as they walked, as if they were trying to find someone.

"What time did you say Jeffrey was supposed to pick Liz up?" Lila demanded. "Two o'clock, wasn't it? It's almost four now. I wonder what they could've been doing all this time."

"I think we're going to find out in a minute," Jessica murmured. "Liz is heading over here. Any second she's going to bump smack into Jeffrey and Olivia."

Sure enough, Elizabeth was just heading back to her towel to put on more sunscreen. She was making her way carefully around the towels and radios, keeping her eyes on the ground so she wouldn't step on anything, and she almost didn't see Jeffrey until she was right on top of him.

"Oh, Jeffrey," she blurted, glaring at him, then at Olivia.

"Liz, don't be mad. We can explain everything," Jeffrey began, sounding guilty and defensive.

Elizabeth frowned. She didn't exactly like his choice of the pronoun *we*, but she certainly didn't plan to let him see that. "There's nothing to explain," she said, bending down to get her beach bag.

"Liz, it was my fault. We went out to Las Palmas to take those photographs, and somehow we got so involved that we completely lost track of time. We didn't realize how late it was getting," Olivia said nervously.

Elizabeth rummaged around in her beach bag, looking for her sunscreen lotion. "There's no reason to apologize," she said in a high voice. "Look, if it took a long time, it took a long time. Why make such a big thing out of it?"

"She's mad, just like you said she would be," Olivia said, looking helplessly at Jeffrey.

Elizabeth glared at her. "I'm not mad. I just figured you were going to take a while, so I got a ride to the beach with Jessica and Cara. Isn't that OK?" She rubbed some sunscreen on her face.

Jessica was listening to this exchange with a combination of interest and alarm. On the one hand it was fascinating to watch her sister fighting with Jeffrey. Jessica had often encouraged Elizabeth to date other guys, not just Jeffrey, so she couldn't help enjoying the battle.

But on the other hand all she could think about was A.J. The more Elizabeth fought with Jeffrey, the more likely she was to keep up her horrible new flirtatious behavior with the redhead. And *that* Jessica did not want to see!

"Liz, you don't sound like yourself. You sound really weird," Jeffrey said, running his hands through his hair and looking at her with complete confusion. "Will you just. . . . Let's go off somewhere for a few minutes and straighten this out. OK? We can't talk here, with everyone listening."

Elizabeth tossed back her hair. "Sorry," she said. "A.J.'s going to take me windsurfing. In fact, he's waiting for me out on the dock. I've got to go."

She spun around and sauntered off, without so much as a glance back at Jeffrey.

He stared after her in anguish. "Oh, God," he moaned, turning back to Olivia. "I *told* you. We should've called the minute we realized we didn't have a watch with us. We should've done something." His face darkened. "I can't believe she's really going windsurfing with A. J. Morgan. He isn't worth it! He's just a dumb jock."

"He is not!" Jessica shrieked.

Lila raised her eyebrows. "Jeffrey," she said calmly, "you can't really blame Liz, can you? How else is she supposed to behave? Especially after Cara told her that she saw you and Olivia in each other's arms in some rest stop off Route Nine!"

"In each other's arms?" Olivia repeated blankly. "What on earth—"

"Don't deny it, Olivia. I was on the way back from the dentist . . . and I pulled into the rest area, where I happened to see Jeffrey's car. And there you were, holding each other—right there for anyone to see!"

"Cara," Olivia said, "I happened to have gotten something in my eye. That's why we pulled in, so Jeffrey could look at it. And that must have been what you saw—Jeffrey holding my head back so he could see if he could find anything."

Everyone was quiet for a minute.

Jeffrey slapped his hand to his forehead. "You mean Liz thinks that Liv and I—that she . . ." He looked horrified. "She thinks we were making out in some rest area? And now she's running around with A.J. to get back at me?"

Cara looked upset, too. "I guess I didn't handle this very well. I should've kept my mouth shut and stayed out of other people's business."

"I don't think everyone should be so upset," Lila said thoughtfully. "It's just a simple misunderstanding. It's not the end of the world. Jeffrey, you're just going to have to do something to make up with Liz. And the sooner you do it the better."

Jeffrey stared disconsolately out to the dock, where A.J. was giving Elizabeth windsurfing lessons. "Yeah. It looks like I'm already too late," he muttered.

"Don't be crazy! Look, maybe you're both too worked up to talk right now." Lila thought it over. "This seems to me like one of those situations when a third party could really help a lot. Why don't you let me talk to Liz? I can explain everything that happened, kind of soothe her a little bit, and then when she's all ready to forgive you, you can do the rest."

"Well, if you really think you can help," Jeffrey said doubtfully.

"Of course I can help! Just watch me!" Lila jumped to her feet, smoothing her metallic suit down over her hips. "I'll be back in five minutes. And if Elizabeth isn't ready to make up by then, I'll—" She stopped. "I'll treat you to a dinner at L'Escalier."

Everyone gasped. L'Escalier was one of the ritziest French restaurants in town. Dinner for two there would cost more money than most of them had to spend in six months!

"This I've got to see," Cara murmured.

Jessica nodded. "Yeah. I'll be amazed if Lila can pull it off," she agreed, watching her friend flounce off in the direction of the dock. "But if she bet on it, she must mean business. Lila may be loaded, but she doesn't lose a bet lightly!"

Everyone waited eagerly for Lila to come back. They could see her, from a distance, approach A.J. and Elizabeth on the dock, touch Elizabeth on the arm, lead her away, and talk animatedly with her. Then Elizabeth started shaking her head and gesturing wildly, and the next minute she marched right back to A.J.

"Doesn't look so good to me," Cara observed wryly. "I hope you're in the mood for a French meal, Jeffrey."

Lila came back, looking concerned. "Well, I guess this may take a little longer than I expected." She patted Jeffrey reassuringly on the arm. "I guess I owe you a dinner, Jeffrey. Maybe we should make it tonight. I think you and I are going to need to discuss strategy. Elizabeth's much more angry than I thought she was."

"Tonight?" Jeffrey frowned. "But Liz and I had plans tonight. We were going to see the new movie at the Valley Cinema." He looked really upset. "Maybe we'd better wait till some other time, Lila."

Lila sighed. "Well, I don't think Liz is counting on going out with you tonight. In fact, from what she just told me, it sounds like she's already made other plans."

Jessica stared at her, an expression of horror on her face.

If Elizabeth had other plans and they didn't include Jeffrey, then who *did* they include?

"OK," Jeffrey said weakly. "If you really think this is the best way to discuss strategy, let's have dinner tonight."

Lila smiled and sat back down on her towel, looking content. She didn't notice the looks she was getting from Jessica and Cara.

"What's the matter with you?" Elizabeth demanded. She was getting dressed in her bedroom, and Jessica, sulking in the chair in the corner, was watching. "I don't see why I shouldn't go out and have a good time. Come on, Jess. You're the one who's always telling me you think it's stupid to get tied down. So all I'm doing is following your advice." She looked in the mirror, made a face, and began brushing her hair furiously.

Jessica rolled her eyes. What a great time for her twin to decide to listen to her advice! And what a great person for her to start flirting with!

"Don't you think A.J.'s nice?" Elizabeth continued.

"Yeah, he seems OK," Jessica said. It took all the effort she could muster to hide the emotions she was feeling. But she managed. She wasn't going to let anyone know how she felt about A.J.—least of all Elizabeth.

"Well, I happen to think he's more than just OK. I think he's smart, funny, good-natured, trustworthy—a real gentleman," Elizabeth said, dabbing perfume behind her ears. "Not like some people!"

"Liz, you haven't even given Jeffrey a chance to explain what happened today," Jessica protested.

"Why should I? I know exactly what happened. He had a chance to spend the day with Olivia, so he did—without even bothering to cancel our plans." Elizabeth selected a pair of earrings and put them on with great care. "Never mind changing my mind, Jess. I'm not going to be the patient girlfriend one minute longer. I'm sick of the whole thing." She studied herself in the mirror. "I haven't looked forward to an evening like tonight in ages!"

Jessica couldn't stand it anymore. "Fine," she said sarcastically, jumping to her feet. "I hope it turns out to be the evening of your dreams." And she stomped off, slamming the door behind her.

As soon as Jessica was gone, Elizabeth reached for a silver chain bracelet, but her fingers were trembling so badly, she couldn't fasten it. Soon her eyes filled with tears, and she could barely see her reflection.

Who am I kidding? she wondered, meeting her blurry glance in the mirror.

She didn't know whether or not she had fooled

her sister, but she certainly hadn't convinced herself.

Olivia Davidson took a deep breath before ringing the Wakefields' door bell. No one answered, and she turned to go to her car. *I should've called,* she told herself with a sigh. She had assumed Elizabeth would be at home. She doubted she had gone out with Jeffrey after the scene on the beach that afternoon. Just then the door opened, and Jessica stuck out her head.

Olivia turned back. "Oh, hi, Jess. Is Liz home?"

Jessica frowned. "Nope, Liz is out with A.J. And as far as I know, Lila is at L'Escalier with Jeffrey. What are *you* doing tonight?"

Olivia sighed. "Well, I was working on some stuff for the literary magazine, but the truth is, I haven't really been able to concentrate. I keep thinking about what happened today, and it's really upsetting me. In fact, I was hoping to find Liz here tonight so I could apologize to her in person. I don't think Lila's idea of acting as go-between is such a great one. I just think it would be better to deal with the problem directly."

Jessica studied her. "Well, you may be right.

But she isn't home. As I said, she's out with A.J.," she repeated. It was torture just saying that, but at this point Jessica was so miserable that she felt some absurd pleasure in talking about it. It was just so unbelieveable. She'd *finally* fallen in love, really, deeply in love, and her own flesh and blood, her own *twin*, had stolen him right out from under her nose.

"Can I come in? I want to ask you what you think about something," Olivia said.

"I guess so. I wasn't doing anything special anyway. Just watching a video."

"Why aren't you out on a date?" Olivia looked at her curiously. "I didn't think Jessica Wakefield *ever* spent Saturday night at home."

"Well, it's kind of a long story." Jessica opened the door. "Come on in. Tell me what's up."

She would rather talk to Olivia than sit around brooding about A.J., Jessica thought. Maybe Olivia would have a plan to get Elizabeth and Jeffrey back together so A.J. would be available again.

"Well, Jessica, I spent a lot of time thinking about this whole mess today, and it seems to me that there may be a way to get to the bottom of it. I want to figure out who started pairing my name with Jeffrey's in the slam books. I just have this feeling that whoever it is, is the one responsible for breaking up Liz and Jeffrey."

Jessica thought this over. "Who would want them to break up?"

"I have no idea. But if we study the slam books and figure out who started the rumor, it will give us something to work with and might even tell us who wanted them apart."

"That's true," Jessica agreed. And whoever had written Olivia and Jeffrey down as a future couple might also be responsible for first pairing up Elizabeth and A.J. She would certainly like to find out who that was so she could take revenge!

"The only thing is, I can't seem to think of a way to find out who could've written it. Can you?"

"No," Jessica said. "It won't be easy. The whole idea behind the slam books is to mix them all up so no one can tell who wrote which entry."

"Yeah," Olivia said softly. "It's kind of irritating. I keep asking myself who could possibly have a reason for breaking up Jeffrey and Liz. And the only person I can come up with is me. But I know I didn't do it. Do you trust me, Jessica? Promise me you do. Promise you know that it wasn't me and that you'll help me find out who really did it." Olivia's eyes filled with tears. "If you don't, Liz is never going to for-

96

give me, and I'll have lost one of the friendships I value most!"

Jessica was thoughtful for a minute. "OK,"
she said at last. "I promise."

As far as she could tell, she had everything to
gain from trying to find the culprit. Because
unless she helped get her sister and Jeffrey back
together, who could tell when she'd have a
chance with A. J. Morgan?

Now all they had to do was figure out who
had written the incriminating entry in the slam
books. And that could take forever!

Nine

Things were incredibly tense between Jessica and Elizabeth all weekend long. Jessica made sure she was in bed Saturday night when her sister got back from her date so she wouldn't have to hear what a wonderful time Elizabeth had had with A.J. And she tried her hardest to avoid her twin on Sunday. Not that it was hard— Elizabeth locked herself in her bedroom for most of the day and wouldn't even come to the phone when Jeffrey called.

"You know," she said to Jessica on Sunday evening, when the twins bumped into each other in the bathroom they shared, "I think you may have been right about Jeffrey. I think he and I got too serious too quickly. I think it's a much better idea to play the field for a while."

Jessica didn't like the way Elizabeth sounded. She thought her voice seemed brittle.

"Well, I certainly can't see the point of rushing right from one heavy relationship to another," Jessica snapped. "Straight from Jeffrey over to A.J. You haven't even had time to breathe between the two."

"What's the matter? You don't think A.J.'s a nice guy?" Elizabeth demanded.

Jessica shrugged. "He's all right. By the way, Jeffrey called three times today. Aren't you going to break down and at least talk things over with him?"

Elizabeth frowned. "I'll see him in school tomorrow. We can talk then."

"Good," Jessica muttered. Maybe tomorrow they would make up and end this nightmare. The whole weekend seemed like a bad dream to Jessica.

Elizabeth woke up on Monday morning feeling terrible. She couldn't believe what a mess the weekend had turned into. Not that she hadn't had fun on Saturday. A.J. was a sweet guy, and she had enjoyed spending time with him. But the role she was playing just wasn't her at all, and she didn't think she could keep it up much longer. The truth was, she felt miserable about her fight with Jeffrey. She needed to talk to him, and she could hardly wait to catch him alone at school. She was sure the minute they saw each other everything would be fine with them.

She took special pains getting dressed and even wore the royal-blue sweater she knew Jeffrey liked. She put her hair back with combs he had given her, then left twenty minutes early for school so she could wait for him outside his homeroom.

By nine o'clock, right before the first bell, Jeffrey still wasn't there. Elizabeth felt extremely anxious as the minutes ticked past. Where was he?

At five past nine he came hurrying in, looking distracted and worried. "Liz!" he exclaimed, stopping short when he saw her. "Where have you been? Don't you know I called you about five times yesterday? Jessica said you wouldn't talk to me, but—"

Elizabeth cut him off. "I was upset. But I know we need to talk. Can we have lunch together today, alone?"

Jeffrey blushed. "You're not going to believe it, but I told Olivia—"

Elizabeth put her hands over her ears. "Cut it out. I can't stand it, Jeffrey."

"No, listen to me! I told her I'd spend my lunch hour printing up the photographs I took for the photo essay. I developed the film yesterday, but I've got to get those prints done for the dummy of the magazine. Mr. Collins wants to know how it's going to look. And I also told Olivia I'd give her a hand with the layouts. She's really swamped, Liz. She needs help."

"What about me?" Elizabeth cried, her eyes filling with tears. "Don't you care about what I need?"

Jeffrey stared at her helplessly. "Of course I do. You know how I feel about you, Liz. Let's talk later. After school—"

"I see," Elizabeth snapped. "You mean after Olivia. Well, if that's how you want to arrange your priorities, that's fine with me."

She didn't give Jeffrey a chance to answer her. She stomped off, blond hair flying and jaw set. That was it. She had come prepared to make up, but Jeffrey obviously had made up his mind. Olivia came first, and Elizabeth wasn't going to put up with that. No way.

She had intended to forget all about A.J., but if Jeffrey didn't care about her anymore, what was to stop her from going after the new boy?

* * *

"Hey, A.J.," Aaron said in a low voice. The two boys were in the corner of the lunchroom, finishing their sandwiches. "Looks like Liz Wakefield is on her way over."

"Oh, wow. Aaron, what is it about these California girls? They're awfully aggressive compared to the girls back in Atlanta." He was quiet for a minute. "In fact, the only girl I've met out here who isn't like that is Jessica." A.J. smiled. "She's more like the kind of girl I'm used to. Quiet, sweet . . . I'd like to get to know her better." He shook his head. "Liz is a little scary to me."

"Well, to tell you the truth, A.J., Liz isn't usually like this. I don't know what's going on between her and Jeffrey."

"Well, she sure isn't acting like she's content with him," A.J. said. "Shh. Here she comes!"

Elizabeth took a deep breath and approached the table. "Hi, Aaron. Hi, A.J. Can I join you?"

"Sure," A.J. said. He pulled up a chair for her.

"I've been looking for you everywhere," Elizabeth said with a big smile. "How can someone as tall as you are be so hard to find?"

Aaron cleared his throat. "I'll just go and get another milk. Can I get anything for you two?"

"No," Elizabeth said silkily. "I have everything I need." She gazed longingly into A.J.'s eyes, and he blushed deeply.

Elizabeth let her fingers drop down near his, but he didn't take the hint. She wondered what she was doing wrong. It had been so long since she had flirted with a guy other than Jeffrey. Maybe she was being too subtle.

"A.J.," she murmured, "I had such a good time with you the other night at the movies. Don't you think you and I should do something like that again—soon?"

"Well, this week is really busy, Liz. I've got practice every night," A.J. said awkwardly.

Elizabeth frowned. Wrong tack again. "Maybe this weekend," she said meaningfully.

A.J. just blushed even more deeply.

"Liz," he said, "excuse me for a second. Uh, I see someone I've got to talk to."

I must really be doing something wrong, Elizabeth thought as she watched A.J. push himself away from the table and stroll across the lunchroom.

"Listen, Jessica," Olivia said in a low voice. "I'm afraid I've got bad news. I've been over this about a million times, and I can't think of one single person who could benefit from putting my name together with Jeffrey's. Can you?"

"No," Jessica said thoughtfully. "I can't."

The two girls were in the student lounge. It was their afternoon study hall, and Olivia had taken a quick break from working on the literary magazine to brainstorm with Jessica about a plausible suspect. But they weren't getting anywhere.

Just then the door to the student lounge opened, and Lila and Jeffrey came in. Lila had her arm tucked possessively through Jeffrey's and was purring consolingly at him. She stopped short when she saw Olivia and Jessica.

"Oh," she said. "I see the lounge is crowded. Let's go to the cafeteria, Jeffrey. We can talk there."

"You can stay here," Olivia said. She was staring hard at Lila. "Can't they, Jess?"

"Of course they can," Jessica said, watching the twosome with fascination.

"I don't think so," Lila said haughtily, her head held high. "Come on, Jeff." She tugged on his arm, and he followed her.

"Jeff?" Jessica repeated blankly. "Since when does Jeffrey let anyone call him Jeff?"

Olivia narrowed her eyes as she watched them disappear down the hallway.

"Jess," she murmured, "something just occurred to me. Didn't Lila lose that bet she made with Jeffrey on Saturday? And didn't that force her to take him out to L'Escalier—for a romantic little tête-à-tête?"

"Yeah," Jessica said. "Not very bright of her. Anyone could have seen she'd lose."

"Right!" Olivia said triumphantly. "Anyone—including Lila. She isn't exactly the sort of girl to throw away a good French meal like that, either."

"What are you trying to get at?" Jessica asked.

"I'm just wondering if Lila is up to something. Look, all of a sudden she wants to be the go-between. She's spending all kinds of time comforting Jeffrey, trying to give him tips on how to make up with Liz. And she's getting pretty darned possessive of his time."

Jessica's eyes widened. "You think Lila's the one who started putting you two down as a couple in the slam books?" She had to admit she hadn't thought of it.

Olivia's eyes were shining. "Of course! It makes perfect sense, Jess. And it explains absolutely everything. Lila liked Jeffrey when he first moved here from Oregon, right? She never really forgave Liz for winning him. So here's a perfect opportunity for her to get him back—and make it look like *I'm* the bad one."

"You're right," Jessica mused. "It's a perfect explanation. I've got to admit I couldn't understand why Lila had suddenly turned into this big mediator. Normally she couldn't care less when a couple is fighting. Your explanation makes a lot of sense."

"Now all we have to do is prove it," Olivia murmured. "I have an idea, but I can't figure out a good reason to do it. If we could collect all the slam books, we could see which ones have Jeffrey and me written down in the Couples of the Future column. You've got to figure that whoever wrote it in the first place wouldn't have written it in her own book."

"That's a great idea! I'll bet you anything Lila doesn't have it in hers." Jessica's eyes shone. "And I bet Lila was the one who first wrote Elizabeth and A.J. in, too."

"OK, now we just have to figure out how we can collect the slam books." Olivia frowned. "I wish I could think of some way—"

"I've got it!" Jessica cried. "I can pretend to be Liz and tell people I'm going to edit them and run a special thing on slam books in the 'Eyes and Ears' column. Doesn't that make sense? People will believe it. It's the sort of thing that the 'Eyes and Ears' column would definitely be interested in."

"Not bad," Olivia admitted. "We'll have to work really fast, though, because if word gets back to Liz, she's going to be furious."

Jessica nodded. "OK, then we'll do it fast. I'll

wear Elizabeth's clothes to school. I'll collect as many slam books as I can in the morning, and you find as many as you can and say you're helping Liz get them for the paper. Then we'll meet at lunch, compare them, and take the evidence to Liz. If Lila is the only one who doesn't have anything in her book about you and Jeffrey, I think we're pretty safe in concluding she's the one who started the rumor."

Olivia nodded. "I think so, too. I just hope it isn't too late for Liz to forgive me and that she and Jeffrey will make up. It's so sad to see them fighting, especially when they're such a good couple."

Jessica nodded. She hoped they made up, too. Elizabeth's little game with A.J. was making her own life miserable. She wanted A.J. for herself!

Ten

Jessica checked her appearance in the mirror in the girls' bathroom after chemistry class. "Not bad," she told herself. She had to admit she looked exactly like Elizabeth. That morning she had borrowed her twin's navy-blue-and-maroon plaid skirt and navy knit sweater after explaining that she was incredibly bored with her own wardrobe. Now she pulled her long hair back into a ponytail and tied it with a dark blue ribbon, just like Elizabeth did. Perfect. No one would be able to tell them apart.

By ten-thirty Jessica had managed to collect a dozen slam books. "It's for *The Oracle*," she explained over and over again.

"OK, but can I have it back by afternoon, Liz?" Robin Wilson asked.

"Sure," Jessica said, feeling a little triumphant glow. This was even easier than she had thought.

"I'm getting tons of them," she hissed to Olivia when she ran into her in the hallway. "I haven't had time to look at them yet. I'm putting them all in my locker. I'll get them before lunch and we can compare notes then."

"Good work," Olivia said. She studied Jessica admiringly. "You look exactly like Liz. Hasn't she wondered why you're dressed like that? In her skirt and sweater?"

"No, I actually *asked* her if I could borrow them, and she let me," Jessica replied.

"Hey," a familiar voice said, "I want to talk to you."

Jessica spun around. Her heart started to pound and her palms went dry. "Uh . . . A.J.," she gasped. Before she could squeak out another word, he grabbed her by the arm and led her off down the hall, with Olivia staring after them.

"I've been looking for you all morning. Where have you been hiding?" A.J. demanded.

Jessica gulped. Should she tell him that she wasn't who he thought she was, or should she just keep her mouth shut and relish being with him?

"It's about time we talked," A.J. went on. "I've been doing a lot of thinking, and I just can't keep quiet anymore. I've been thinking about *you*," he added.

Jessica stared at the floor and shuffled from one foot to the other. She couldn't stand this. She was going to have to tell him the truth.

"A.J., I'm not who you think I am," she said softly.

A.J. still had his hand on her arm. He propelled her into the student lounge and shut the door. "What do you mean?" he asked, facing her squarely.

Jessica gulped. "I'm not Elizabeth. That's what I mean."

"I see." A.J. crossed his arms. "And why do you think I thought you were Elizabeth?"

"Because—" Jessica stared. "You mean you didn't? You thought I was Jessica?"

"Now, look, you've got to be one or the other," A.J. said with a laugh. "I happen to have seen Elizabeth twice this morning already. She's wearing a pink sweater, so you can't be her. And unless there're *three* of you, or unless your sister's in the habit of changing clothes every hour on the hour, I just assumed you were Jessica. Was I right?"

"You were right," Jessica whispered. She

couldn't believe how shy she felt around him. "But why did you want to see me?"

"Why?" A.J. looked down at her with a fond smile. "Because I think you're great, that's why. And I want to get to know you better."

Jessica's heart was pounding so hard, she thought she was going to faint. "Me? Not Liz?"

A.J. frowned. "Well, you're both nice. But that sister of yours is awfully flirtatious. Boy, Jessica, I sure don't understand how anyone could've put you down as Biggest Flirt in those slam books. I don't want to say anything bad about your sister, but, well, you're so shy compared to her!"

"Oh, well—" Jessica was about to defend herself when A.J. cut her off.

"And that's why I like you. I like girls who are a little bit on the shy side. It may be old-fashioned of me, but I like to be the one who chases the girl, not the other way around."

Jessica stared at him. If anyone else had said that, she would have burst out laughing. But since it was A.J. and since she was madly in love with him, she looked demure and nodded sweetly. "Oh, I agree with you. Totally," she said. "I hate it when girls chase guys."

A.J. smiled. "You're the kind of girl who really likes to listen to a guy. You're not aggressive. You're sweet, gentle . . . the sort of girl I can completely trust."

Jessica nodded, fascinated with this description of herself. She didn't bother to ask how A.J. had determined all this about her when they had barely been introduced. She liked hearing all these wonderful things about herself, even though none of them sounded very familiar. Best of all, she loved basking in A.J.'s attention. And she wanted to stay there forever.

"So that's why I think you and I should get to know each other better, Jessica," A.J. concluded. He leaned over and touched her gently on the cheek. "And I mean it."

Jessica smiled modestly. "Oh, A.J.," she said with a little giggle.

She was so thrilled that he had finally noticed her that she forgot all about the fact that she wasn't exactly what he thought she was. She wasn't one bit shy or sweet or demure at all.

But that didn't matter for now. The important thing was that A.J. liked her. They would have plenty of time, later on, to get to know each other better. And once he found out what she was *really* like, he'd care for her even more!

"OK," Olivia said grimly, arranging the slam books in stacks. "I managed to get ten. And you got twenty-one. That means thirty-one slam books to go through."

Olivia and Jessica were in the student lounge with the door closed. Jessica guarded the door, making sure no one came in and saw what they were doing while Olivia leafed through the books.

"This is Robin Wilson's," she said, holding up the first slam book. "Page thirty-four, under Crystal Ball, New Couples—the first entry is Olivia and Jeffrey."

"Go on," Jessica said.

"Maria's book, Olivia and Jeffrey. Elizabeth's book, Olivia and Jeffrey. DeeDee Gordon's, same thing." Olivia went through the books as quickly as she could. "Let's see. Mine, yes. Cara's, yes. Sandra's, Jeanie's, ditto."

In ten minutes Olivia had gone through the entire stack of slam books. Every single one had an entry under Couples of the Future predicting that Olivia and Jeffrey would get together.

Then they came to the last book in the pile— Lila Fowler's.

"My fingers are trembling," Olivia said in a hoarse voice. "I hope this works, Jess. It just has to!"

"Hurry up," Jessica said. She opened the door, peeked outside, and closed it again. "Lila happens to be heading right for the lounge!"

Olivia flipped quickly through the pages. Under the Crystal Ball category, she found the page she was looking for. Olivia and Jeffrey's names were not there.

"Jess, come here!" Olivia cried.

But Jessica was cramming the slam books into her knapsack with lightning speed. "Hurry, up," she cried. "Give me that, Olivia!"

Olivia handed her the incriminating slam book just as the door opened and Lila strolled in.

"Excuse me," she said. "Am I interrupting something?" She stared at Jessica. "Jessica? Why are you dressed like Elizabeth?"

Jessica gulped. "I—uh, was just sick of all my own clothes, that's all."

Lila shrugged. "You ought to borrow something of mine, then. That's really a little too preppy for you, Jess." She glanced at Olivia. "What's going on in here? You two look like I just caught you cheating on an exam or something."

"We were just. . . ." Olivia's voice trailed off as she looked pleadingly at Jessica to help her out.

But Jessica was too angry with Lila to care much about inventing an excuse. She couldn't believe Lila had really been the culprit. That meant it was Lila's fault that this whole mess had happened, and if it weren't for Lila, Jessica thought, she and A.J. would probably be going together already.

"We were just conducting a little survey, that's all," Jessica said coldly. "Come on, Olivia. We need to show Elizabeth what we found."

She gave Lila a meaningful look, but Lila didn't seem to notice. "Poor Liz," she said. "She and Jeffrey really don't seem to be ironing out their problems, do they? I don't know about you guys, but I think they're having a real communication problem. In fact, I was just trying to find Jeffrey. I wanted to tell him that I've thought it over, and I really don't see any point in his trying to make up with her anymore."

Olivia and Jessica looked at each other, and Jessica rolled her eyes. "I'm sure that's good advice, Li," she said sarcastically. "Come on, Olivia. Let's go find Liz."

They didn't have any time to lose. Who knew what kind of sneaky, conniving thing Lila would tell Jeffrey? If they wanted to get to Elizabeth before Lila ruined her romance completely, they were going to have to move fast!

Elizabeth was in the middle of editing a story for *The Oracle* when Olivia and Jessica burst into the office, their arms filled with slam books.

"Liz! Stop what you're doing and listen to

us!" Jessica cried, pulling the door shut behind her and dumping the slam books down on the desk in front of her. "We have to tell you what Lila did," Jessica said hastily.

"Let me explain," Olivia broke in. "Liz, I've been going absolutely nuts for the past few days. I couldn't stand thinking that you thought I was trying to break you and Jeffrey up. You know how much I care about you and how much respect I have for you as a friend! I would never in a million years try to ruin your relationship. In fact, I think you and Jeffrey make a great couple."

Elizabeth stared at the heap of slam books in front of her. "I don't think I really get it yet," she said, "but maybe this is all going to make some kind of sense in a couple of minutes. What's going on here? Why are all these slam books on my desk?"

"That's why I'm wearing your skirt. I had to, so people would think I was you and they'd let me collect them," Jessica said breathlessly.

"We wanted to get to the bottom of this rumor that Jeffrey and I were going to be a new couple," Olivia added. "So we collected all the slam books and went through them. We figured that whoever had started the idea wouldn't have bothered to write the entry in her own book."

Elizabeth stared at her. "I hadn't thought of that," she said slowly. "What did you guys find?"

"Look." Olivia started opening books at random, showing Elizabeth the entries. "Every single one of these books has the entry in it—I mean, all but one. Now, maybe we're wrong, but we think it looks kind of suspicious. In fact—"

Just then the door to the *Oracle* office opened, and Lila stuck her head inside. "Hi, guys," she said cheerfully. "Has anyone seen Jeffrey? I've been trying to find him everywhere."

Her eye fell on the pile of slam books, and a funny expression crossed her face.

"Lila," Jessica said sweetly, "why don't you come on in and sit down? We were just talking about you."

"That's OK," Lila said hastily. "I'm actually in kind of a hurry."

And with that she closed the door and went charging off.

"As we were saying," Olivia said with a smile, "only one of the books doesn't have the entry. And that one happens to belong to Lila Fowler."

"Lila?" Elizabeth's eyebrows shot up. "But why would . . . I mean, what possible advantage would. . . ." Her eyes narrowed as she stared at Lila's slam book. "You mean Lila wanted to break Jeffrey and me up, and that's why she put this entry in all the slam books?"

"We're not saying that," Jessica said. "All we're saying is that it looks like Lila's the one who did it. And all of a sudden Lila seems awfully interested in consoling Jeffrey. She seems to be making it her business to give him all sorts of advice now that you two aren't on speaking terms."

"And she just told us that she thinks you two are having such serious problems that she feels obligated to tell him to give up on you," Olivia added.

"Boy," Elizabeth said with a groan. "I feel like a major jerk. Olivia, I can't believe how badly I've treated you! I convinced myself you were trying to steal him from me, when I should have known you'd never do anything like that in a million years!"

Olivia was quiet for a minute. "I'm sorry if I gave you any reason to mistrust me, Elizabeth. I *do* like Jeffrey, a lot, but only as a friend. Since Roger and I have broken up, I've been feeling so sensitive and vulnerable. It's helped me to spend time with Jeffrey. And when he wanted to use me as a model in his photo essay, I was really flattered. So maybe there was a grain of truth in your suspicions. But I certainly never liked him as anything more than a friend. And I

119

know for a fact he's so in love with you that *no one* can ever lure him away." Olivia laughed. "Not even Lila!"

Elizabeth shook her head. "I've acted like such an idiot. I just hope you'll forgive me, Olivia. And I hope Jeffrey will be willing to listen to my apology."

Olivia smiled. "I'm sure he will," she said softly. She put her hand on Elizabeth's. "Look, Roger and I reached the point where we really couldn't talk anymore and couldn't have a good time with each other, either. Don't let that happen to you and Jeffrey. Promise me you'll try to make up with him."

Elizabeth blinked to hold back her tears. "I just hope I'm not too late," she whispered.

Eleven

Elizabeth tried to find Jeffrey everywhere. He wasn't in the lunchroom or the student lounge. He wasn't in the darkroom, and he wasn't in the gym kicking a soccer ball around. Finally she remembered. He was doing a special review in his chemistry class. It was an informal meeting, conducted by a senior honors student, but Elizabeth knew she shouldn't interrupt it.

She had to get a message to him, though. She couldn't wait any longer.

She sat down outside the chemistry classroom, tore a sheet of notebook paper out of her notebook, and wrote:

1. Most Sorry—Elizabeth Wakefield
2. Most Eager to Make Up—Elizabeth Wakefield
3. Feeling Like the Biggest Jerk—Elizabeth Wakefield
4. Jumped to the Most Ridiculous Conclusions—Elizabeth Wakefield
5. Most in Love with Her Boyfriend—Elizabeth Wakefield
6. Most Willing to Talk About What She Did Wrong and Why— Elizabeth Wakefield
7. Most Likely to be Waiting for You When You Get Out of the Lab—Elizabeth Wakefield

She folded up the piece of paper, wrote Jeffrey's name on the outside, and knocked on the door. When the student leading the review came outside, Elizabeth, keeping her face very straight, said she had an urgent note for Jeffrey French.

"No problem. I'll give it to him," the student said. "We're actually taking a break now anyway."

To Elizabeth it seemed like ages before Jeffrey came outside. But the big smile on his face told her that it had been worth waiting.

"Listen, stranger," he said, putting his arm around her. "How am I supposed to become a brilliant chemist unless I have all my mental powers focused on my experiments?"

Elizabeth giggled. "I didn't mean to distract you. It's just that I happen to have acted incredibly badly, and I wanted the chance to tell you how sorry I am."

"The chance is all yours," Jeffrey said, pulling her close to him and kissing her on top of her head. "Do you know I've been going crazy for the past few days?"

"You're not the only one. I can't stand fighting with you. It makes me feel like the whole world has turned upside down." Suddenly Elizabeth was serious. "Jeffrey, please forgive me!" she cried. "I can't believe how stupid I've been. How could I have possibly thought that you liked Olivia?"

Jeffrey looked serious, too. "It wasn't just you, Liz. I was doing something wrong, too. I should've been much more considerate of your feelings. If I'd had any idea how you felt, I would never have gone out to the canyon on Saturday."

Elizabeth sighed. "When you hear who first put that entry about you and Olivia in the slam books, you're never going to forgive me for making such a big deal out of it."

"What do you mean?"

"Oh, Jeffrey. This whole thing was manufactured by Lila." Elizabeth shook her head sadly. "Apparently her plan was to start a fight between us, leap in to console you and give you all sorts of advice, and then, as the saying goes, catch you on the rebound."

Jeffrey looked stricken. "You mean that's why Lila's been dragging me out to dinner and insisting on having all these tedious conversations about you and me for the past few days?"

"I guess so." Elizabeth studied him closely. "You didn't even suspect that's what she was up to?"

"No, it never crossed my mind." Jeffrey tightened his arm around Elizabeth. "I missed you so much, I wasn't doing a whole lot of thinking." He frowned. "And what about this guy, A.J.? What does he have to do with all this?"

"Oh . . ." Elizabeth blushed. "I was, uh, kind of flirting with him, Jeffrey. I was feeling hurt, so—I—I—" She started to giggle. "I chased him a little bit. But you don't have to worry. He was running the other way the whole time! I think I scared him to death. Aaron Dallas says that he likes shy girls, like the ones back home in Atlanta."

Jeffrey glowered. "Good. I don't want you flirting with him, and I don't want Lila flirting with me. I just want you and me to be together. Understood?"

Elizabeth nodded. "Understood," she murmured.

She hadn't been this happy in days. It felt wonderful to be in Jeffrey's arms again, and she didn't plan to let go of him for a very long time.

"So you and Jeffrey made up, and you and Olivia made up," Jessica said thoughtfully. The twins were sitting out by the pool in their backyard, catching some sun before the last rays disappeared. It was Tuesday afternoon, and Elizabeth was filling her sister in on everything that had happened.

"Yeah. There's only one thing I still don't understand." Elizabeth frowned. "I can see why Lila was acting funny. But what about you? What did anyone do to get you as upset as you've been for the past few days? Ever since Friday night it seems like I can't do anything without making you furious at me."

Jessica was quiet for a minute. "Well," she said at last, "the truth is, I didn't exactly like it when you started flirting with A.J."

"With A.—" Elizabeth broke off. Suddenly her face cleared. "I don't believe it," she cried. "You mean you've been interested in A.J. all this time and you never said anything to me about it?"

Jessica fidgeted uncomfortably. "That's right. I didn't feel like telling anyone how I felt about him. This is different, Liz. It isn't like anything that's ever happened to me before."

Elizabeth stared at her, her eyes wide. "It sure *sounds* different. I've never heard you like this before, Jess." She studied her twin closely. "Does A.J. know that you like him?"

"I—well, I think so. I don't know." Jessica shook her head. "I think maybe he likes me a little. He told me today. . . ." She turned bright red.

Elizabeth started laughing. "Wow. This is hysterical. A true comedy of errors. Here I was flirting with A.J. when I wasn't even interested in him, and you were furious with me because you like him and you never even told me."

Jessica nodded. "But it's OK. A.J. doesn't like flirtatious girls anyway. He told me so."

Elizabeth stopped laughing. "He doesn't—Jessica, what does that mean? How in the world is he supposed to like you if he doesn't like flirtatious girls?"

Jessica made a face. "I'm not flirtatious anymore, Liz. Haven't you heard a single word I've said? I happen to have changed."

"Oh," Elizabeth murmured. "I see. And A.J. likes the new you better than the old you?"

"It isn't like that. You're making it sound contrived," Jessica said angrily. "I happen to be really and truly in love this time. Big-time love. This is it, Liz. I'm through with flirting and going after a different guy every week."

"Well," Elizabeth said dubiously, "that sounds great and all, but I wonder. . . . I don't know, it just seems that it's incredibly important to be able to tell a boyfriend anything, to be able to be yourself with him no matter what."

Jessica was in a trance. "He's so sweet, Liz. He has eyes that just make me totally melt. And when he looks at me, it's like . . ." Her voice trailed off.

Elizabeth laughed. "Sounds like love, all right." She looked at her sister with concern. "I just hope he isn't going to cramp your style, Jess. You're not exactly one of those shy, retiring southern girls I've heard he misses so much."

Jessica hadn't heard a single word her sister said. She was imagining what it would feel like the first time A.J. took her in his arms and kissed her.

Olivia hurried up to Elizabeth Wednesday morning at school. "Have you and Jessica thought up anything yet? You know, for the get-back-at-Lila-Fowler scheme?"

Elizabeth shook her head. "Not yet. I'm trying as hard as I can. But Jessica's a little out of commission. I don't know whether or not you've noticed, but Jessica's in love." Elizabeth laughed. "I've actually never seen a case this bad in my whole life. She isn't really among the world of the living. Trying to talk to her is like trying to send a telegram to Mars."

Olivia giggled. "So she's really nutso about A.J., huh?"

"*Nutso*," Elizabeth agreed, "is exactly the right word to describe it."

"Well, listen. Now that I've got a dummy of the magazine together, Mr. Collins wants to have a little party after school today—you know, to drum up interest for the magazine. Hopefully a few people will offer to help out, once they've seen it. I wanted you and Jeffrey to come. Do you want to ask Jessica and A.J., too? Maybe we can brainstorm with them about how to get back at Lila."

"That sounds good. I know I can come, and I know Jeffrey will want to. But it's hard to know anymore about Jessica!"

Jessica, as it turned out, was more than happy to come. A.J., she informed her twin, *liked* literary magazines. More to the point, he liked girls who liked literary magazines, girls who were studious, hardworking, shy—sort of like Elizabeth.

And like Jessica, now.

Elizabeth thought about this as she strolled down the hall. She was so deep in thought, she almost didn't notice A.J. until she was right next to him.

"Oh, A.J.!" she exclaimed. "Just the person I wanted to see!"

A.J. paled and drew back. "Liz . . ." he began.

Elizabeth giggled. "You think I'm going to start chasing you again, don't you?"

A.J. was still alarmed. "You're not going to, are you? Liz, I'm sorry. I'm just not used to girls like you. I think I need someone a little, you know, more subdued." He grinned. "More like your sister."

Elizabeth tried to hide a smile. "Yes, well, I'm sure that's true." Let him find out on his own what Jessica was really like, she thought. If he thought Jessica was subdued, well, he was in for a big surprise. "I want to apologize for the way I've been behaving. I—" She blushed. "Well, actually, I'm usually not like that. So aggressive, I mean. It's just that Jeffrey and I were having a little misunderstanding, and I was kind of trying to make him jealous."

A.J. looked intrigued. "Liz, I forgive you completely. And I'm glad we can be friends." He looked at her with interest. "Boy, you and Jess sure are different. I bet she'd never cook up a scheme like that in a million years!"

Elizabeth bit her lip. "Uh, yeah. I guess you're right," she murmured.

She had to stare at the floor so she didn't give away her surprise. She didn't know how her sister had done it, but A. J. Morgan seemed to think Jessica was somebody else completely!

The party for the new magazine was being held in the *Oracle* office at four o'clock. Mr. Collins had strung banners above Olivia's desk and hung up a big sign that said "Congratulations!" He had also supplied platters of cookies and lots of soft drinks. It wasn't a large party—only about a dozen people—but Elizabeth could tell how much it meant to Olivia.

"I'm so glad you guys came." Olivia gave her a big smile. "What do you think of the cover Jeffrey designed?"

Elizabeth inspected the sample cover. Jeffrey's photograph of a tree just budding into leaf was beautiful. And she liked the magazine's title: *Visions*. "It looks great, Olivia. You should be proud of yourself."

Olivia patted her on the arm. "I'm just glad we're friends again."

Elizabeth nodded seriously. "Me, too. I've really learned my lesson, Olivia. I guess if you can't trust someone and talk things through, then you're bound to believe any rumor that comes along without even bothering to think about it first."

Olivia's eyebrows raised. "Hey, here comes your sister."

Elizabeth turned around. Sure enough, Jessica was just coming in the door, with her arm linked through A.J.'s. Jessica *looked* the same, but Elizabeth couldn't get over how quiet and subdued her sister seemed. Was this really the same twin she had lived with all her life?

"Oh, Olivia, what a wonderful cover!" Jessica exclaimed in a voice twice as sweet and half the volume of her usual voice.

"Thanks," Olivia said, trying to hide a smile. "I didn't know you were that interested in literary magazines, Jess."

Jessica looked distressed. "Oh, I've always liked literature. Poetry, stories, you know. All that." She looked hastily at A.J. to make sure he was listening. A.J. was beaming with pride.

"Jessica's a writer herself," he told Olivia. "She writes children's stories. Don't you, Jessica?"

"Uh, well, I'm about to start one," Jessica said quickly, avoiding her sister's penetrating gaze.

"You're kidding. Well, you'll have to submit something to the magazine," Olivia said. The next minute Mr. Collins called her over and she moved away, leaving Elizabeth staring at her twin sister.

Jessica? Writing a children's story? This was news. Elizabeth had a feeling the only fiction her sister had created was the fiction she'd been feeding A.J. She wasn't exactly sure what was going on, but Jessica was obviously trying to invent a new image.

A.J. had fallen for it, too. He didn't let Jessica out of his sight once.

Elizabeth couldn't help having some misgivings. She wasn't sure who A.J. was interested in. But if it was Jessica, he would find out soon that this sweet, demure girl had nothing to do with the real Jessica Wakefield!

Twelve

"OK," Olivia whispered to Amy Sutton. "Give me your slam book, Amy."

"I don't get it. What's all the mystery?" Amy demanded.

"Never mind," Elizabeth said. "Olivia and I just have a new category we want to put in. Don't we, Olivia?"

Olivia grinned. In blue ink she wrote "Class Sneak." And right underneath it, "Lila Fowler."

"Now let me fill in yours," Elizabeth said to Robin Wilson.

Before long the slam books were all jumbled up, and the group of girls sitting together in the lunchroom were busy reading out loud from other sections.

"Here's a good one. Fastest Personality Change —Jessica Wakefield." Amy giggled. "That's for sure! What on earth has come over that girl? She skipped cheerleading practice yesterday to go to that literary magazine party. I mean, no offense, Olivia, but since when has Jessica been interested in literature? I always thought her idea of literature was mail-order catalogs!"

Lila, who had just come over with her tray, raised one eyebrow. "What's so funny? Can I sit down?"

"Sure, Lila," Elizabeth said, winking at Olivia. "We were just reading out loud from the slam books. Hey," Robin said, "there's a new category in mine!"

"Mine, too!" Amy said.

"Mine, too," Cara chimed in. "Class Sneak."

"And there's only one name written in underneath it—Lila Fowler," Amy said. She turned to Lila, her expression puzzled. "Lila Fowler—class sneak? What on earth can that mean?"

Lila stared at Elizabeth, then at Olivia. A deep blush burned across her face.

"I haven't the faintest idea," she said haughtily. "I think I'm going to sit over there with Maria," she added, sweeping off.

Olivia and Elizabeth burst into fits of giggles. They refused to explain to any of the others what the new category meant. They didn't have to. They'd gotten what they wanted, and Lila knew that they had figured out what she had tried to do.

They decided they would just leave it at that. And for the rest of the day everyone wanted to know why Lila was being called Class Sneak. Let Lila explain if she wanted to!

"Elizabeth?" Jessica knocked softly on her sister's door that night. "Can I come in?"

"Sure!" Elizabeth set down the book she was reading. "What is it, Jess?"

Jessica picked the book up. "*Tender Is the Night* by F. Scott Fitzgerald," she read. "Is this any good?"

Elizabeth smiled. "Yes. It's wonderful," she said. "But you can't tell me you came in here to talk about Fitzgerald."

Jessica shrugged. "Look, Liz. You like to read and everything. Maybe you can help me figure something out."

"What?" Elizabeth asked. Her twin seemed upset.

"Well, I was just wondering." Jessica fidgeted with her hair. "I mean, to me, reading's just something you do when you have to. I could never figure out what fun it was to read big fat novels like you do. But I've been thinking I might, you know, want to learn more about that kind of stuff. Like poetry." She blushed. "A.J. likes poetry, and I told him I did, too."

Elizabeth stared at her. "Why?"

"What do you mean, why? Because *he* does, that's why! I may not know anything about literature, but I know about this kind of thing." Jessica looked determined. "Liz, I want you to help me. Tell me what kind of stuff to read, and I'll read it."

"Look, Jess. It's not that I don't think it's great that you're getting interested in new things. Especially in poetry and literature. It's just—" Elizabeth frowned. "Well, you know what you've always said about girls who get obsessed with stuff just because they're going out with some guy who likes whatever it is." She shook her head. "Can't you just be yourself with A.J.?"

Jessica stared at her. "I *am* being myself. I happen to have a whole lot of interests you don't know anything about, that's all. Come on, Liz. Tell me what sort of stuff I should be reading."

Elizabeth shrugged. "Well, if you're really going to go through with it, you might as well read this." She handed her sister her favorite poetry anthology. "Just read through it and see who you like. Try to develop your own taste."

Jessica looked horrified. "Liz, this thing's enormous! I can't read all the way through it. Tell me who's good and I'll just read their poems," she begged. She started to flip through the pages. "What about Emily Dickinson? Is she good? Or John Keats?"

Elizabeth looked at her in despair. "They're both good," she said. "Jessica, why don't you just give up? I notice you missed cheerleading practice," she added.

"I went to the library. A.J. hasn't said he doesn't like cheerleaders, but I can tell he likes girls who are . . . you know, smart, hardworking. Like you," Jessica concluded, still flipping through the anthology.

Elizabeth sighed. She didn't like the sound of this. *Then how in the world is he ever going to like you, Jess?*

She didn't dare say so to Jessica, because it was obvious her twin was too excited about A.J. to listen. But Elizabeth was beginning to think her sister was headed for disaster!

Will Jessica convince A.J. that she's the girl for him? Find out in Sweet Valley High #49, **PLAYING FOR KEEPS.**

YOUR OWN

SWEET VALLEY HIGH

SLAM BOOK!

If you've read *Slambook Fever*, Sweet Valley High #48, you know that slam books are the rage at Sweet Valley High. Now *you* can have a slam book of your own! Make up your own categories, such as "Biggest Jock" or "Best Looking," and have your friends fill in the rest! There's a four-page calendar, horoscopes and questions most asked by Sweet Valley readers with answers from Elizabeth and Jessica

Watch for FRANCINE PASCAL'S SWEET VALLEY HIGH SLAM BOOK, on sale in September. It's a must for SWEET VALLEY fans!

☐ 05496-1 FRANCINE PASCAL'S SWEET VALLEY
HIGH SLAM BOOK
Laurie Pascal Wenk   **$3.50**